WILD IRISH EYES

BOOK 2 IN THE MYSTIC COVE SERIES

TRICIA O'MALLEY

LOVEWRITE PUBLISHING

WILD IRISH EYES

BOOK 2 IN THE MYSTIC COVE SERIES

The longest road out is the shortest road home - Irish Proverb

CHAPTER 1

$\mathcal{C}$AIT GALLAGHER HUMMED along to the traditional Irish music that played softly through the speakers hidden deep in the corners of the pub that she owned in Grace's Cove, a small village set on the shores of Southern Ireland. Cait admired the gleam of the dark wood that accented all of her whimsical Irish décor as she wiped down a table. Content, and happy that the rehearsal dinner for Keelin and Flynn had gone so beautifully, Cait let her guard down and set her mind to wander.

"I bet she's good in bed. She's so tiny that I could throw her over my shoulder and drag her out of here."

Cait straightened as Patrick's voice shot through her mind. Forcing herself to keep all emotion from her face, she bent to wipe the table once more before turning towards the bar where Patrick, her new bartender, washed glasses in the new glass cleaner she had just purchased. Even if she couldn't read minds, the hunger she saw in young Patrick's eyes was unmistakable. He blushed when Cait glanced his way and, dipping his head, he focused on the task at hand. Cait blew out a small breath and ran a hand through her short, curly mop of hair. At just over five feet tall, Cait was indeed tiny. A slim frame, short hair, and greenish-gold eyes completed the package and often had her being mistaken for a little girl. Those who knew her never made that mistake. As a pub owner, Cait had a commanding presence, a rigid backbone, and a healthy dose of risk-taking. She'd been known to break up more than her fair share of brawls. Typically though, it took little more than her raised voice to stop an argument in its tracks.

Cait kept an eye on Patrick as she moved around the pub. A recent hire, he was just eighteen years old and full of testosterone and angst. With his dark hair and gray eyes, Cait imagined that he had already cajoled more than one girl into his bed. Smiling, she shook her head at the urgency of youth and reminded herself to keep her mental shields up, as she would probably hear more than she needed to from Patrick if she wasn't careful. Cait shot him a friendly smile as she ducked under the pass-through behind the long wood bar that framed rows of glass shelves hung in front of a gilded mirror. Liquor bottles of all shapes and sizes clustered the shelves. Cait prided herself on stocking more than just the average fare and enjoyed offering a variety of drink choices. She bent to tuck her cleaning supplies beneath the counter. Turning, she slammed into Patrick's chest and stepped back involuntarily as he caged her with his arms.

Cait took a deep breath as her pulse picked up its pace. Blowing out her breath, she met Patrick's eyes.

"I think about you. A lot." Patrick's words sent an

involuntary shudder through Cait and she realized that maybe she should have listened a little more closely to Patrick's thoughts. Allowing her shields to drop, Cait did a quick scan of Patrick's mind. She breathed a sigh of relief as she found a healthy dose of lust but no intent to harm. Cait reached up and patted Patrick's arm.

"Patrick, I'm almost ten years older than you. While I'm flattered, you need to find a woman your own age to date." Cait smiled gently at him. She gasped as he wrapped his arms around her and pressed a passionate kiss to her lips. Cait let out a soft squeak before she contemplated how to break the kiss without bruising his fragile ego.

"What's going on here?"

A voice sliced across the pub and Cait tried not to groan as Patrick stepped hurriedly back from her. Cait knew that voice. Its owner had starred in more than one of her most decadent fantasies.

"Have I interrupted something?" Shane MacAuliffe stepped up to the bar and leaned casually against the railing as his brown eyes coolly assessed the situation. His lanky frame belied a whipcord strength that Cait had seen exhibited on several occasions.

"No, you haven't. Right, Patrick?" Cait turned and crossed her arms, staring down the young man. Patrick's cheeks turned pink and he ducked his head, nodding at the floor.

"Why don't you take the kitchen bin out and finish cleaning up in there?" Cait suggested, and Patrick nodded, not meeting her eyes. He ducked quickly beneath the pass-through and all but ran for the kitchen, the door swinging wildly behind him. Cait huffed out a sigh and turned to face Shane. She was dying to read his thoughts but her own code of honor prevented her from doing so. She'd have to deal with this like a regular person.

Cait allowed her eyes to scan Shane. His casually proper attire was something that she knew he took time with, just as she knew that he drove into Dublin for his haircuts. His blond hair and stubborn jaw made him an attractive, if not an interesting man to look at. The unofficial mayor of Grace's Cove, Shane owned more than half of the commercial real estate buildings, including the one that housed her pub. Still, that didn't mean it was okay for him be here after hours, Cait thought. Deciding to take the offensive, she glared at him.

"And what are you doing, sneaking in here after hours?"

Shane raised an eyebrow at her and Cait was startled to see anger lying beneath the cool surface of his calm façade.

"I own the place, remember?"

Cait blew out a breath and turned to finish cleaning the glasses. The task gave her something else to focus on and forced her to keep her mouth from saying something stupid like, "Take me." Cait did a mental eye roll. She promised herself that one day she would get over this insatiable crush that she had on her landlord.

"Yes, sir, I remember." Cait infused her words with bitter sarcasm. He always hated it when she called him *sir*.

"Knock it off. What are you doing messing with that kid? He's too young for you," Shane said bitterly as he ducked behind the bar and helped himself to a Harp.

"Make yourself at home, there," Cait said.

"Put it on my house account. Now, answer my question."

Cait finished washing her hands and dried them carefully on a bar rag that hung in front of her. Part of her was gleeful that Shane cared and part of her was infuriated that he thought that she was too old for Patrick.

"My love life is my own. Thanks for asking though."

Cait gasped as Shane stepped towards her, pressing her small body back against the bar. She allowed her eyes to trail up his chest, past his clenched jaw, to where his deep brown eyes were murderous. It was so rare for Shane to show emotion like this that Cait found herself trembling against him.

"Your love life? You're sleeping with him? What kind of boss are you?"

Shock hit Cait at his words and a warm flush of anger and embarrassment shot through her.

Her voice shook and she skewered Shane with a glare.

"I'm the best kind of boss. One that knows what she wants and gets it. No matter what. And at this moment that would be you...leaving my pub. Now."

Shane took a deep breath and stepped back from her. Cait felt oddly bereft at the absence of his heat. She held his eyes as he nodded once at her and ducked beneath the pass-through.

"Excuse me, then. I'll just leave you to your business. I'm sure that Patrick can walk you home instead." Shane slammed through the front door and Cait brought her trembling head to the bar, allowing the smooth wood to cool the heat of her forehead. What had just happened? Cait needed a moment to breathe.

"Um, I'd be happy to walk you home."

Cait stayed where she was as Patrick's voice greeted her from across the room. If she knew her town, this would be the gossip on everyone's lips over breakfast tomorrow.

"No, thank you, Patrick. Come here, we need to talk."

Patrick walked to the other side of the bar and met her eyes, the naked hunger in his eyes softening her stance. Though Cait felt the pleasure of being wanted wash through her, she also knew that Shane was right. Patrick was not only too young for her, but he was also her employee.

She pulled out two shot glasses and filled them with a splash of Tullamore Dew. She slid one across to Patrick.

"Here's the deal, Patrick. I'm flattered that you are attracted to me. But, at your age, you'll find someone else in under a week. And you should...you should be out testing the waters and seeing what you do and don't like. Not only am I not the one for you, it also goes against my rules and my ethics to sleep with an employee. You do a good job here and I want to keep you on. But, I'm going to have to ask you never to make a pass at me again. Do you think that you can handle that?" Cait said firmly, her eyes never wavering from the young man's face. Patrick took a deep breath and nodded once before breaking into a smile.

"So, we're okay?"

Cait smiled at him and held up her shot glass. "Slàinte." They clinked glasses and she allowed the warm burn of the whiskey to slip down her throat. The heat only seemed to fuel her anger at Shane but she kept a cool demeanor as she and Patrick chatted about the rehearsal dinner they'd hosted at the pub earlier that evening. Cait went around and flicked off lights and tried not to think about why Shane had come to the pub tonight. Instead, she thought about Keelin and Flynn's wedding tomorrow. Cait was going solo as she was a bridesmaid in the wedding, but that didn't mean she wouldn't be able to mingle with the guests. Knowing that Flynn owned restaurants across Ireland had led Cait to hope that maybe she'd meet a new man, one not ensconced in Grace's Cove. One…that wasn't Shane. With a sigh, she ushered Patrick from the pub and locked the door behind her, pocketing her keys smoothly.

Her small flat was only a few blocks away and made her commute convenient, though she often wished that she wasn't so accessible to all of her employees. Cait supposed that that was the drawback of owning your own business. She laughed at herself as she walked the quiet street towards her building. She loved owning a pub in Grace's Cove. Rumored to be a mystical town, the cove drew curiosity seekers from around the world. Tourism was a big business in Grace's Cove and Gallagher's Pub was at the heart of it. So what if people thought the cove was enchanted? They wouldn't be far wrong, Cait thought. Rumors held that legendary pirate queen, Grace O'Malley, had protected it as her last resting place and that very few were allowed to enter the cove without being harmed. Whispers of powers passed down through Grace's bloodline heightened the reputation of the town. It was good for business and business was booming.

She wouldn't change it for the world, Cait thought, and smiled at the sleepy town.

CHAPTER 2

*S*HANE'S HEADLIGHTS SLICED through the inky blackness that could only come with living far from city lights. As he drove the cliff road towards his home in the hills, Shane's stomach churned. Why had he gone to the pub tonight? Seeing Patrick pressing his lips against Cait's had awakened a primal beast in him. It had taken everything Shane had to remain calm and not send Patrick sailing over the bar.

Shane slammed his fist into the steering wheel as he pulled into his driveway. Turning the car off, he sat for a moment and took a calming breath. Closing his eyes, he remembered his one taste of Cait.

He didn't even know how it had happened. A seemingly innocuous conversation about renting property had turned into a fight about money and class wars. Shane had been so frustrated with Cait that he had done the only thing that he could think of to shut her up and had kissed her.

Shane groaned as his body tightened in response to thinking about Cait's hot lips and trim body. He'd lost himself for a moment in her kiss…her heat. She'd been like a knife to the gut, all passion and resistance. Her lips had been eager and hot against his own and had Keelin not interrupted them, Shane wondered where it would have gone.

Since then, it seemed as though Cait had been avoiding him. Shane wondered if he had misread her signals through the past year. He'd been convinced that she was interested in him. Shane couldn't remember a time when Cait hadn't been at the forefront of his thoughts. He'd watched as she'd overcome a difficult upbringing to make a smashing success of her pub. That was part of what appealed to Shane: Cait had as much grit as she did heart.

He was on unsure footing here, and that made Shane uneasy. He liked to know where he stood with people. Doing so had made him a successful businessman both in Grace's Cove and through his real-estate holdings in Galway. Cait confused him. She pushed him and pulled him in. Shaking his head, Shane got out of his car. Maybe it was time to see where her interest really stood.

CHAPTER 3

"$\mathcal{D}$O YOU HAVE more concealer?" Cait asked over her shoulder as she peered into the mirror. Keelin's grandmother, Fiona, was having the women get ready at her cottage in the hills outside Grace's Cove. Dark circles ringed her eyes. A fitful night of sleep mixed with excitement for her friend's wedding had left Cait looking haggard. Keelin's head appeared over her shoulder in the mirror and Cait felt her heart clench.

"Oh...oh, you're just stunning," Cait gasped and turned to hug her friend. Keelin's strawberry-blonde hair was twisted back in an intricate half braid and then left to tumble over her shoulders. Her brandy brown eyes were expertly shadowed and a flush of excitement filled her cheeks. Keelin clenched Cait close and, letting down her mental guard, Cait allowed Keelin's happiness to pour through her. When Keelin had first come to Ireland over the summer from Boston, they had initially forged a tentative friendship. After discovering that they were both descendants of the mighty Grace O'Malley and that they both shared special gifts, their friendship had been forever cemented. Though Keelin's gifts ran more along the lines of healing and foreseeing the future, Cait had identified with her feelings of otherworldliness instantly. It wasn't easy to explain to others that she had a little extra something special, Cait thought. In fact, she rarely told anyone about herself.

Feeling a little weepy, Cait stepped back before she got both of them crying. Keelin ran her hand down Cait's arm.

"What's wrong, sweetie? I can feel it," Keelin asked her softly. The room was filled with the bustle of women getting ready and Keelin was trying to be discreet. Cait just shook her head at her.

"Honestly, I don't even know if I could explain if I tried. So, don't worry. For another time. We'll have a pint." Cait smiled at her friend and Keelin nodded.

"Okay, I'm holding you to that. Now, let's get you into makeup and then into your dress."

"Thank God you got someone to do makeup. These bags under my eyes are ridiculous."

"Don't worry, we will have you prettied up in no time, ya old hag." Keelin laughed at her and poked her in the arm. Cait smiled and dutifully went into the bedroom, where the makeup and hair command stations were set up. She raced to the makeup girl and threw her arms around her.

"Save me, oh wise one. Work your magic on me!" Cait demanded dramatically. The makeup girl laughed and shoved her into the seat.

"Oh dear, we do have some work to do. You really need to sleep before events like these," Susan, the owner of the local salon and today's "makeup girl" said as she squinted her eyes at Cait.

"Well, some of us work until the wee hours of the morning, might I remind you?" Cait said huffily. It seemed everyone was in agreement on how crappy she looked. Lovely, Cait mused. Then she reminded herself that today wasn't about her and she let the happiness course through her again. Cait held still as Susan muttered over her face, applying creams and shadows.

"There, you're gorgeous. Now, off to hair," Susan demanded.

"Ha, what are they going to do with this mop of mine?" Cait asked as she switched chairs and one of Susan's girls began to run her hands through Cait's hair. Her curls came to just below her chin and Cait wondered what they could manage to change about it.

"Your hair is lovely. Such a nice deep brown and it holds curls really well," the stylist murmured as she began to run a curling iron through Cait's hair to touch up some of her curls. In a matter of moments, the stylist patted her shoulders.

"All done. It doesn't take much to make you look fantastic," she said as she brushed Cait's shoulders and pulled her to look in the mirror.

"Thanks, ladies, you are good for my ego," Cait laughed at them and then turned to examine herself in the mirror. She let out a small gasp at the changes they had elicited in her appearance. Her hair was arranged in a sexy tousle of curls around her head but the stylist had parted it to the far left so a slice of hair cut across her face and made her look edgy…even sexy, Cait thought. The makeup was subtle yet her eyes seemed huge in her face. The green of her irises seemed to glow against her skin and Cait wasn't sure if it was the touch of color on her cheeks or the whip of cat-eye that the eyeliner gave her but she felt feline, exceptional, and sexy.

Turning, she looked at Susan. "I'll buy all of the products you used on me today."

Susan laughed and nodded. "Just add it to my tab at the pub. I'll come by this week and show you how to do what I did."

Cait nodded and turned back to the mirror. She couldn't stop staring at herself. Making a mental note that it wouldn't hurt for her to put more time and effort into her appearance, Cait moved to where her dress hung, wrapped in plastic. As she struggled with getting the plastic off, Cait reviewed her daily wardrobe. She was a jeans-and-a-tank-top type of girl. Her slim build didn't lend itself to sexy dresses. She had long ago accepted that she wouldn't have bombshell curves like Keelin. And she was okay with that—mostly, she thought. Pulling the dress from the hanger, she stepped into the bathroom.

Cait sighed as she pulled the strapless dress past her shoulders and over the soft curve of her hips. At least Keelin had chosen something that would flatter her, was all Cait could think. She'd been surprised at Keelin's restraint with the wedding. The Irish were known to go a little overboard when planning their nuptials. Cait shuddered as she thought about the hundreds of euros she had spent on hideous dresses and hairpieces. Keelin had opted for simplicity and Cait couldn't love her more for that decision. Straightening, she eased the zipper up her back, though she'd need help with the last few inches. Cait turned towards the mirror and a broad smile broke out on her face.

The lavender dress clung in all the right places and seemed to give her the illusion of curves that Cait was quite certain she didn't have. A sweetheart neckline accented her strong shoulders and a dip in the waist show-cased her flat stomach. Turning, Cait examined the back of the dress and smiled as the expertly tailored dress concealed her one bane of annoyance...a very round bum. Keelin swore she should be proud of it but Cait hated how hard it was to find jeans. With a slim build and small waist, most jeans didn't account for a sizeable bottom. This dress made her look proportionate and lovely. With a final deep breath, she whisked out to the main room to help the bride finish getting ready.

CHAPTER 4

*M*ERE MOMENTS LATER, Cait took another deep breath before she stepped from the door of Fiona's cottage. Keelin had been determined to get married in the hills overlooking Grace's Cove and had brought her vision to life in the simplest way possible. An aisle lined with tin buckets of wildflowers led through rows of bushels of hay covered in cloth. An arbor built of branches with wildflowers woven through stood at the end of the aisle. Flynn stood beneath the arbor in a simply cut tuxedo that outlined his strong shoulders nicely. Cait gulped; she couldn't wait until he saw Keelin. As the music struck up, Cait braced herself; it was almost time to go.

First down the aisle were the couple's dogs, Ronan and Teagan. The crowd laughed as the dogs, festooned in a bow and a bowtie respectively, marched down the aisle to meet Flynn. Cait laughed; it was a perfect beginning to the wedding. Ronan, Keelin's dog, had been a gift to her from Flynn and had played a major part in the couple's courtship. Blinking back a sudden sheen of tears, Cait stepped onto the aisle with her groomsman, none other than Flynn's cousin and her employee, Patrick.

She glanced at Patrick and saw his cheeks flush as he looked at her. Probably still embarrassed from last night, Cait thought, and shot him a warm smile to let him know that everything was okay. He breathed out a sigh and walked to her, holding his arm out for her to grasp. Together, they stepped lightly down the aisle, smiling at family and friends. Cait swept her eyes through the crowd and landed on Shane's face, looking murderous. She stumbled a bit and Patrick steadied her. Forcing herself to keep a smile on her face, Cait lifted her chin and smiled at Shane. He nodded at her once before turning to say something to a lovely blonde woman sitting next to him. Cait felt the inside of her stomach curl with bitterness as Shane leaned close and whispered in the blonde's ear, making her laugh. Cait had never seen the blonde before and assumed that it must be one of Shane's big-city girls.

What was he doing here with her? Cait took a deep breath to steady herself. It wasn't like her and Shane had anything, she reminded herself. They'd shared one kiss. Cait did a mental eye roll as she thought about the kiss. The power of it had been like a punch to her heart. Since then, she'd spent countless nights agonizing over what the kiss had meant. If she was honest with herself, Shane scared her. His world was so different from hers. He was all fancy businessman and she was a hardworking grunt just trying to make her dream of owning a successful pub come to fruition. And, because the promise of his kiss had rocked her so deeply, Cait had kept her distance from him since.

Refusing to let Shane ruin this beautiful day, she shot Patrick a dazzling smile and continued to the end of the aisle, where she gave Flynn a wink before stepping to her side of the arbor.

Cait turned to watch as Keelin made her way from the cottage. Her friend had picked the perfect wedding dress for this venue, as well as for her body. A deep V of lace dipped from her shoulders, nipped in at the waist and then wove in ripples over her generous hips. The dress was sexy, subtle, and perfect for an outdoor wedding. Keelin tossed her hair back and shot a grin to Flynn before she had Fiona walk her down the aisle. Cait shot a quick glance at Flynn and saw him wipe a tear from his eye. It was all she could do not to cry herself and Cait blinked back the tears that threatened to fill her eyes. Fiona smiled broadly as she walked slowly with Keelin, nodding at the guests. Cait wondered if Keelin had even bothered to try and find her long-lost father and invite him to the wedding. Knowing that it was a touchy subject for her friend, she had never broached the subject. She saw that Keelin's half-sister, Aislinn, and half-brother, Colin, were in the audience. The three siblings had slowly been working on their relationship.

Cait kept a smile on her face and let the vows of love wash over her. Helpless not to, she met Shane's eyes as promises of everlasting love were made. Shane stared at her, enigmatic. Cait blinked before she accidentally let down her guards and read his mind. It would do no good to know what he was thinking. Ultimately, it was the actions of a man that showed his true feelings. And so far, Shane had done little to prove that he was truly interested in her.

For months now, they had been in a sort of dance with each other, Cait thought furiously. It was always one step forward, three steps back. The kiss had changed everything for her. The only thing that Cait was sure of at this point was that she was powerfully attracted to Shane. His feelings for her continued to remain a mystery.

Moments later, the crowd let out a cheer as Flynn dipped Keelin for their first kiss as a newly married couple. Cait whooped and threw her flowers in the air, ecstatic for her friend. She all but danced down the aisle, ready for a good party. It wasn't often that she took weekend nights off from work but this occasion had certainly called for it.

Cait stood dutifully for the wedding pictures that followed. She was glad when they didn't venture down the cliffs into Grace's Cove. For years now, Cait had avoided the cove. She had mixed feelings over its powers and couldn't explain the strange pull that the deep blue waters held for her. Keelin had tried to broach the subject with her on several occasions but Cait had always turned the conversation in a new direction. Grace's Cove made her nervous and had haunted her dreams many a night. Tearing her eyes from the water, Cait smiled at the photographer and waited patiently for the all clear. She wanted a drink.

Once done with pictures, Cait danced up the hillside to where a large tent was set up along with a small dance floor. Music, as much a part of Ireland as whiskey and brown bread, was already in full force and many couples tried their hands at some Irish step dancing on the floor. Cait shot a grin at some friends, and helpless not to, went to check on the food preparations. She snagged a cider from the bar on the way and made her way to the secondary tent where Fiona oversaw the food preparation with an eagle eye. Coming close to the old woman, she wrapped her hand around her shoulders and took a sip of the crisp cider.

"Ah, this is perfect. All of it."

"It will be if I have anything to say about it," Fiona said and shot an order at one of the line cooks to turn the meat before it browned too much on one side. The cook smiled good-naturedly and nodded back at Fiona.

"She's a beautiful bride. They are the perfect couple." Cait couldn't conceal the note of wistfulness that snuck into her voice. Fiona turned and eyed her shrewdly.

"I see that Shane brought a date," Fiona said casually and turned back to keep an eye on the food prep.

"So?"

"So? What are you going to do about it?" Fiona asked pointedly.

"Nothing. Not a damn thing. I'm going to enjoy my friend's wedding is what I am going to do," Cait said determinedly.

"Mmhmm. Why don't you ask him to dance?"

"Nope. Not happening. He's mad at me. I all but kicked him out of the pub last night," Cait admitted.

"Hmm. And why is that?"

"He overstepped his boundaries," Cait said evasively.

Fiona kept silent and finally Cait sighed and broke. Quickly, she filled Fiona in on the scene in the pub the night before.

"Interesting. One would say that Shane is quite interested. Isn't that your read?"

Cait grabbed Fiona's arm and dragged her a few steps further from the cooks and dropped her voice to a whisper.

"I don't read him. Ever."

"Can't you?" Fiona cocked her head, confused.

"No, I certainly can. I just refuse to. I...I just want something like this to develop, ah, normally. I feel like if I read his thoughts I would have an edge on him. It isn't fair," Cait declared fiercely.

Fiona smiled at Cait and leaned up to press her weathered lips to Cait's smooth cheek.

"You've a heart of gold, Cait Gallagher. I'm as proud of you as if you were one of my own."

Cait blushed at Fiona's words and ducked her head. "It's hard. I really want to," she whispered.

"That's normal. You choose to use your gifts wisely. Come see me next week. I think it is time we started to investigate the depths of what you can do."

Cait felt a tremor shoot through her. She felt like she'd come to terms with her gift as it was. She controlled it and had built her own shields and boundaries to manage it. Fear gripped her at the thought of examining it. Would it be like opening the floodgates?

"I...I don't think that I am ready for that," Cait admitted.

"Nobody is, my dear. Nobody ever is. To ignore it would be careless though. Just look at Margaret," Fiona said as she nodded to her daughter.

Cait turned to watch Margaret, Keelin's mother, who had flown from Boston for the wedding. It was her first time coming home since she had left Ireland and her gifts before Keelin had been born. Dropping her shields, Cait reached out with her mind to do a quick scan of Margaret's. She found a warmth and lightheartedness there that was deeply covered by bitterness, sadness, and a touch of regret. As if sensing the mental intrusion, Margaret turned and made eye contact with Cait. Cait broke away and turned to help the caterers with the first order of food.

Fiona eyed her daughter sadly. "She's deeply unhappy, you know. No amount of material possessions nor her diehard work ethic and fabulous career will make up for her disconnection with her soul. You're heading that way yourself. Come, next week." This time it was a command and Cait sighed heavily.

Just what she needed, Cait thought. She had enough on her mind with running a fulltime business as well as trying not to think about Shane. The last thing she wanted was to rip the Band-Aid off the gaping sore of her magickal powers. Cait smiled and waved to a friend and strode across the grass to give her a hug. Within moments, Cait was swept into the crowd of mostly familiar faces.

Within the hour, the crowd was feasting on some of the finest Irish fare that Cait had enjoyed in years. She groaned as she pushed her plate away and laid a hand on her stomach. Turning, she laughed at Keelin and rolled her eyes. Keelin leaned close and grabbed her arm.

"Who is the bitch that's with Shane?" Keelin asked.

Cait huffed out a laugh and raised her eyebrows at Keelin. "Should you be swearing on your wedding day?"

"It's my day, I can do what I want." Keelin raised her head haughtily.

"I don't know. And I don't care," Cait said as she stuck her chin up.

"Liar. Ask him to dance."

"I will do no such thing. I…listen, I'll tell you later. But I kind of kicked him out of the pub last night. I promise. We'll talk. Not now. Smile, Fiona is about to toast you," Cait said to distract her and Keelin smiled but pinched her arm and gave her a warning look. Cait suspected that she would be getting a phone call within a day or two to discuss full details.

Moments later, the band struck up in song and the guests all stood to clear the tables and make room on the dance floor. Cait tapped her foot to the beat and leaned back in her chair to smile at the couples already dancing on the floor. A mingling of ages from a small toddler bouncing erratically to a couple who had recently cele-brated their 60th wedding anniversary stepped to the lively Irish tune. The sun had set an hour ago and the light of soft lanterns illuminated the tent. Cait clapped as Keelin and Flynn stepped onto the floor for their first dance. She got up to join the ring around them and cheered loudly when Flynn dipped Keelin for a lingering kiss. Cait caught Shane's eyes across from the happy couple. His gaze was mulish and Cait lifted her chin and turned to the old man next to her.

"Mr. Murray, can you keep up with me?" Cait loved to dance and the old man laughed at her.

"I think the question is if you can keep up with me, Cait Gallagher."

Mr. Murray swept her onto the floor and soon the tent was a blur of movement and laughter. Cait's wine glass was repeatedly refilled and she drank with abandon, as she wasn't driving this evening. The night took on a warm haze, and Cait felt her cheeks heat with excitement and exertion. Thanking her latest dance partner, she made a move to find water when a slow dance started.

Patrick stepped forward and stopped her from leaving the floor.

"Can I have this dance?"

Cait gave him a meaningful look. Helpless not to, she glanced across the room and saw Shane standing with the blonde next to the dance floor, whispering into her ear.

"Fine, but this means nothing. I swear that I will fire you in a heartbeat if you try anything funny," Cait whispered to Patrick and saw a huge smile light the young man's face.

"I promise. I'm just trying to make that girl jealous," Patrick said and nodded to where a pretty brunette stood talking to a group of guys. Cait saw the girl glance quickly at Patrick and Cait had to laugh. Funny how things worked sometimes.

"Okay, fair enough. But...I still think you should plow through that group of guys and take her onto the dance floor," Cait advised as Patrick led her to the floor and pulled her into his arms.

"Oh, I plan to. First, I need to see if she even notices me," Patrick said.

Cait didn't have to read the girl's mind to know that she was interested in Patrick, but feeling loose, she allowed her shields down and took a quick scan of her mind. A veil of red jealously hit her and Cait huffed out a small laugh.

"Oh, yeah, you'll be just fine. I saw her looking at you," Cait said quickly. She smiled brilliantly up at the young man and allowed him to pull her a little closer. It was nice to dance closely with someone, Cait thought, and purposely kept her eyes on Patrick's face. Her insides churned as she thought about Shane leaving with the cute blonde. She was everything that Cait wasn't. Blonde, tall, with curves to make every man drool. Cait tried to tell herself that she had her own charm but next to the blonde, Cait was quite certain she looked like a little boy. Patrick pulled her a little closer and her body began to warm against him. The combination of too much wine, Patrick's expert dancing, and the closeness of the crowd was making her dizzy. The song ended shortly and Patrick stepped back, lifting her hand for a gentlemanly kiss.

"Go get her, tiger," Cait whispered. She needed a moment of fresh air and quickly slipped through the crowd to leave the tent. Without hesitation, she stripped off her nice shoes and walked into the fields, allowing the cool grass to brush against her legs. The night was clear and a soft breeze blew in from the ocean. Light from the full moon kissed the hills and emblazoned a trail across the ocean to the cove. Entranced, Cait quickly crossed the field until she stood close to the edge of the jagged cliffs that hugged the waters of the cove. The water here was dark and Cait looked up again at the bright moon. Though her brain was fuzzy with wine, she was fairly certain that there should be some sort of reflection off the water below.

A shiver ran through Cait. There was something about the cove that made her want to dive from the cliffs and swim deep into the dark water. The waters held a siren song for Cait and she'd always avoided the cove for that very reason. Cait lived her life by some very strict and necessary rules. Answering a siren's call didn't fall into those categories for her.

A hand grabbed her arm and wrenched her back from the edge. Cait shrieked as she was pulled against what felt like a brick wall of muscle. Without thinking, she turned and slapped the person.

"What the hell are you doing, Cait?" Shane all but shouted at her.

"I'm catching my breath from dancing, if you must know," Cait shouted right back at him. Her chest heaved and she tried to wrench her arm from his hand.

"Catching your breath two steps from the edge of the cliff after how many glasses of wine? I never thought you could be this stupid," Shane said angrily as he dragged her further from the cliff's edge.

"Stupid? Stupid! Who are you calling stupid? And how do you know how much I've been drinking anyway?"

"Because I've been watching you. I've always watched you," Shane said bitterly as he dragged her across the grass.

"Stop. Just stop. What does that even mean?" Cait demanded of Shane and slammed her hand on his chest to get him to look at her.

"Again? Can you be this stupid?" Shane said angrily. Keeping her arm in his hand, he wrenched Cait to his chest and captured her lips in a blistering kiss.

Cait's brain short wired and all of her senses went on high alert. Shane's kiss was demanding and Cait moaned into his mouth. Taking it as an invitation, Shane slipped his tongue between her lips. Cait shivered as heat pooled low in her stomach and she melted into his chest. His kiss was intoxicating, a promise and a threat in one. She stumbled backwards as he broke the kiss abruptly and pushed her from him.

"Stay away from the edge," Shane ordered and with a heated look, he stormed away from Cait.

Cait held her hands to her lips and found her mouth gaping open. She shut it quickly and turned her back on Shane's retreating figure to stare blindly at the cove. Her heart pounded in her chest as she tried to understand the absolute rightness of that kiss. Cait wasn't sure if she'd left one edge to find herself poised on the brink of another.

Cait gasped and a shiver of fear rippled through her as a soft blue glow emanated from the cove's waters. Her heart skipped a beat and she turned to scream to Shane but no words came out. Stunned, she watched as the glow dimmed the further Shane walked away.

"That's it, no more wine for me," Cait declared and turned her back on the cove.

CHAPTER 5

"LOOK ALIVE THERE, Ms. Gallagher," Cait's kitchen chef said as once again she found herself blocking the door to the kitchen. Cait rolled her eyes and stepped aside. She made her way to the bar and decided that she needed an Irish coffee to nurse her hangover from too much wine. After her kiss with Shane last night she had returned to the wedding and immediately downed another glass. Shane must have left after their heated kiss and she was spared from seeing him dance with the blonde again.

Cait had slept poorly and what few dreams she did have were littered with images of glowing blue water. She'd woken with a headache and in a surly mood. Cait bent to pull the heavy cream from the cooler and whipped it quickly before pouring it on her coffee. She added a gentle amount of whiskey and hoped that the bite of Irish would take the edge off of her dulled senses.

Settling in at a table by the bar, Cait reviewed stacks of invoices that needed to be paid as well as her inventory list. *Money comes in and out it goes*, she mulled. Pride kept her in business as much as did a healthy following of patrons. She'd never be filthy rich, but finally, in her third year in business, Cait felt like she could breathe a little easier. Her tiny nest egg was slowly growing. Someday she'd buy this building from Shane and own the pub outright.

Thoughts of Shane hurt her head and she gulped angrily at her coffee. The hot liquid stung her tongue and she swore before slamming the cup down on the table. Burying her face in her hands she took a moment to breathe.

"Looking good, cousin." Aislinn's warm voice cut over Cait and she peeked from between her fingers and groaned. Aislinn, Keelin's half-sister and a second cousin of Cait's, looked the picture of health and Cait knew that she'd had more than her fair share of wine the evening before.

"How come you look so great?" Cait demanded.

Aislinn smiled peacefully and pulled up a stool next to Cait. "Fiona gave me a little something to help."

"She did? Why didn't she give me anything?" Cait said, righteously angry.

"Apparently she decided that you needed to feel your pain today." Aislinn's eyes laughed at her and she reached out to run a hand over Cait's arm.

"Of course, another lesson from the great Fiona," Cait mumbled and then shut her mouth and looked around. It wouldn't do to be heard speaking poorly of Fiona and Cait knew that it was just her bad mood that had her being cranky.

"What's troubling you? I can see it's more than just the hangover. What happened with Shane?" Aislinn asked directly, unerringly narrowing in on the exact cause of Cait's problems.

"God, how do you do that?" Cait asked grumpily.

"How can you pluck thoughts from people's heads?" Aislinn asked serenely. Aislinn had her own gifts. She'd been blessed with being able to see auras and to read people's feelings. Another thing that Cait didn't care to examine too closely. Which reminded her…

"Fiona wants me to come to the house this week to work on my skills," Cait said, deftly changing the subject.

"Ah, and how do you feel about that?"

"I don't know. I feel like…I'm fine. That I'm where I am supposed to be with my ability. So why can't I just stay with that?"

"Because everything changes. Nothing stays the same. Do you think your gift or your understanding of it will stay the same the rest of your life? It is fluid and ever changing. I think that this might be exactly what you do need."

Cait sighed and rubbed her hands over her eyes again before taking a timid sip of the now-cooling coffee.

"Okay, I get that. But I don't want to face this. It scares me."

"Why? It is who you are." Aislinn tilted her head at Cait and examined her face closely.

"But…but, why? Why me? Why us? Why can't we be normal?" Cait asked stubbornly. She struggled with the ability to understand her extra talents as a gift.

"Why would you want to be?" Aislinn said carefully and Cait brought her head up to look at her in surprise.

"I guess that I've never considered that."

"Well, my friend, maybe it is time to think of these talents of ours as a gift...not a curse."

"I saw the cove glow from within last night," Cait rushed out on a breath. Silence greeted her and she met Aislinn's eyes.

"Did you? How interesting," Aislinn said.

"Yes, I think so. Yes, I definitely did. Or it was the wine."

"And what were you doing down there if I may ask?"

"I just needed a moment to step away from the dancing. I walked to the edge...almost without thinking. I swear that place pulls me to it," Cait said as she shredded a paper napkin on the table in front of her.

"I understand. It pulls me too." Aislinn nodded at her.

"It does?"

"Of course. Our bloodline rests there. That is powerful magick. But...were you alone?" Aislinn said, returning to the point.

"Yes, I walked there alone," Cait said carefully.

"And did you stay alone?" Aislinn said with a laugh; Cait knew she could read right through her.

"No, Shane came and pulled me back from the ledge all dramatic like."

"He did? He left his date to go after you." Aislinn cocked an eyebrow and waited for Cait to go on.

Cait blew out a breath. "Ah, well, we yelled at each other and then he kissed me." Cait gulped as heat flooded her body again as she thought about his kiss.

"Did he now? Isn't that wonderful?" Aislinn smiled like a cat that had just been given a full bowl of cream.

"Is it? Because it felt like it was wonderful and frustrating and angry all at the same time. And then he called me stupid and left!" Cait threw up her hands.

"Sounds wonderful and angsty. A perfect kiss." Aislinn nodded her approval and picked up Cait's coffee for a sip.

"What do I do? Where do I go from here?" Cait asked.

"Well, to Fiona of course. Ask her about the cove. She'll know what to say," Aislinn said.

"No, I meant about Shane, not my gift."

"I know," Aislinn said, and rose to give Cait a hug before trailing casually from the bar.

Well, what was that supposed to mean? Feeling even more confused than before and not having any answers about the glowing of the cove, Cait took a deep breath and forced herself to focus on the numbers before her. She'd go to see Fiona on Monday, her official day off. She needed to get her feet back under her for now.

CHAPTER 6

*C*AIT JOSTLED THE bag of food that she had brought for Fiona as she struggled to exit gracefully from her car. Not that Fiona deserved the fresh baked goods that she had picked up on the way out of town, Cait thought. She was still a little miffed that Aislinn had been given a hangover cure while she hadn't received one.

Excited barks greeted her and Cait grinned as Ronan, Keelin's dog, whipped around the corner of the cottage. Cait knew that Ronan still preferred the cottage to Flynn's massive estate just over the hills. Testing herself, she reached out with her mind to scan the dog's thoughts.

"Happy you're here. Hi, Hi, Hi. Play?"

Cait laughed at Ronan and, kneeling down, she wrapped her arms around the Irish setter's neck. "No time to play, but I didn't forget to bring you a treat."

Cait reached into her bag and brought out a pupcake. The bakery made a special cupcake just for dogs and she knew that Ronan loved the special treat. Ronan jumped and did two excited spins before sitting eagerly in front of

Cait. Cait pulled the wrapping from the pupcake and held it out to Ronan. He took it delicately from her hand and then raced across the grass to find the perfect spot to eat it.

"You certainly have a way with animals." Fiona's voice cut over Cait and she straightened, bringing the bag with her.

"Yeah, well, any dog loves you if you bring a treat for them." Cait shrugged her shoulders and moved to give the old woman a hug. Fiona, though diminutive in size, had a presence that was larger than life. Known around Ireland as a healer of great power, just as many people revered her as feared her. Fiona had been instrumental in helping Cait to understand the weird thoughts that would pop into her head as a child. In some respects, Fiona had become her real family.

"Methinks it is more than the pupcake…" Fiona trailed off with a smile and ushered Cait into her stone cottage. The door opened directly into the main room and a huge wooden table dominated the space. To the left, a small kitchen sink was framed by large windows that overlooked the hills and Grace's Cove far below. On the right, a small alcove housed two rocking chairs and a charming wood-burning stove. Doors led from the main room into two bedrooms and a pantry. Cait allowed her gaze to trail over the long wall of shelves that held hundreds of glass bottles, steel canisters, and burlap bags. Each one was meticu-lously labeled and Cait knew that Fiona used these herbs religiously in her healings. Keelin was following in her footsteps. Between centuries-old herbal remedies and an otherworldly gift for healing with their hands, the pair made a powerful healing duo.

"Speaking of treats, I brought you some, though I shouldn't have, old woman," Cait said as she put the bag on the table and turned to glare at Fiona.

"Hmpfh," Fiona said and snatched the bag from the table, digging around until she found her favorite lemon poppy seed muffins. "And why am I undeserving of my favorite muffins?"

Cait laughed at Fiona's raised eyebrow.

"Because you took Aislinn's hangover away but not mine!"

"Ahh, yes. Well, sometimes you need to feel the consequences of your actions," Fiona said and took the bag to empty the muffins into a small basket that she lined with a dishtowel.

Cait sighed. It has always been like this between them. Fiona had all but acted as a stand-in mother when Sarah refused to acknowledge Cait's gift when she was growing up.

Cait sat at the long table, eyeing the large pile of wedding presents that were clustered on one end.

"Have you heard from Keelin?"

"Yes, they are having a lovely time on the Aran Islands. It seems that now Keelin has embraced her Irish heritage, she never wants to leave."

"What about Margaret?" Cait asked and reached for a muffin. The lemon scent teased her nose and she could all but taste the muffin without having taken a bite.

"She left today. Though I'm unclear if she is going back to Boston or not," Fiona said.

Cait raised an eyebrow at her in question.

"Did you see Keelin's father last night? He kept to the background."

"I didn't at that. Did she invite him?"

"She did, yes. But they have a lot to work out. But... hm, I get the sense that Margaret may not be heading back to Boston," Fiona said.

"Do you think she'll stay here? For him?"

Fiona shrugged her shoulders and gave a casual wave of her hand. "Affairs of the heart...you never know where they will lead one."

"Does she use her power?" Cait asked curiously.

"We spent a long time talking yesterday. I don't know if she will ever accept who she is though she is starting to come around to Keelin living here." Fiona shrugged her shoulders sadly.

"I know that you wish she would stay," Cait said. Margaret was Fiona's only daughter.

"I do. I love her. But...just maybe, the tide is changing with Margaret. We'll see. But everyone has his or her own path, Cait. I can't force her to find her path." Fiona turned her eyes on Cait.

"Isn't that what you are trying to do with me?" Cait demanded churlishly.

"Is that what you think that I am doing?" Fiona raised an eyebrow at Cait.

Cait hung her head and tore her muffin to pieces on her plate. "I don't know."

"While I do think that the time has come for you to fully understand your gifts, you absolutely can walk out the door right now and go on living as you have been." Fiona gestured towards the door.

Cait felt her heart sink a bit. Though worry gnawed at her stomach, she kept thinking about what Aislinn had said about viewing their talents as gifts and something to be excited about. Perhaps it was time to stop rejecting that side of herself, after all. Never one to step away from a challenge, Cait made a decision.

"No. I want to learn more. I...well, this all makes me kind of uncomfortable. I've done my best to just keep the shields up that you taught me. Perhaps it is time to delve deeper into what I can do."

A wide smile brightened Fiona's face and she reached out to clasp Cait's hand.

"You're stubborn, but I've dealt with worse," Fiona said. Cait knew that she spoke of Margaret.

"Sooo, how does this all get started?"

"Why don't we go for a walk and I'll give you your first history lesson," Fiona said as she rose and cleared the plates.

Together they stepped from the cottage and into the bright sunshine. It was one of those perfect summer days in Ireland, though Cait knew that the weather could change in a heartbeat. At the moment, a light breeze teased Cait's hair and the azure sky was clear. Smiling, Cait took a deep breath and followed Fiona on a path that cut directly across the blindingly green hills that rolled towards the cliffs that guarded Grace's Cove. Fiona let out a sharp whistle and a bark responded. Cait laughed as Ronan tore across the hill in a flat-out run, his ears streaming behind him in the wind. Teagan, Flynn's dog, followed closely behind Ronan.

"Oh, aren't you both the mighty beasts?" Cait called to

them as they circled and barked around them. The dogs raced joyously through the grass and Cait smiled after them before continuing to follow Fiona. She stiffened as the old woman led her closer to the cove and a whisper of trepidation slipped through her.

"Are we going to the cove?" Cait called to Fiona.

"Aye, we are."

The old woman continued nimbly along the path and Cait picked up her pace to keep up with her. She really didn't want to go into the cove and wished that Fiona could just tell her what she needed to know from here.

They reached the edge of the rock ledges and Cait steeled herself to look down into the cove. A seemingly normal, and stunningly beautiful, beach scene greeted her. Crystalline blue water filled the perfect half-circle cove, and high rock walls hugged the water, shrouding it in privacy. A long sand beach lay below them. It was the kind of beach that Cait would expect to see packed with people. Startling in its beauty, it begged for families to camp out with their kids and play in the water. Yet, it was very few people that ventured to the cove. Too many had died here. Too many had been harmed here. They felt it, she thought. There was no way that the average person couldn't feel that there was something off with this beach.

"Let's go," Fiona ordered and picked her way along the path that switchbacked down the cliff to land at the beach.

Cait hesitated and felt the brush of Ronan's fur against her leg. He looked up at her for a moment before following closely on Fiona's heels. With a sigh, Cait began the descent. She was surprised at Fiona's dexterity on the hike down but she supposed that she shouldn't have been. The old woman had walked these hills since she was a child. Cait watched as she gathered snippets of flowers on the way down and wondered what remedy she would make with them. As they drew closer to the beach, Cait shivered as she felt the hum of power brush against her skin.

Fiona stopped at the base of the path and waited for Cait to catch up.

"Have you been down here before?" Fiona asked Cait.

"Just once. It wasn't a good experience," Cait said mildly. It had been more than not a good experience, she thought. She'd almost drowned. It had been a stupid dare from her childhood friends to run down and grab a rock from the beach and bring it back. She'd been almost to the path when a rogue wave had caught her and pulled her back. Cait shuddered as she remembered the wave tossing her like a rag doll across the sand before somehow spitting her out back at the path. She hadn't looked back and she and her friends had run all the way to the top of the path. Cait hadn't returned to the beach since. One thing you could say about Cait was that she wasn't stupid. Well, at least most people would say that, Cait thought, and kicked at the sand.

"Pay attention," Fiona said fiercely and Cait snapped back to the present. Fiona held wildflowers in her hands and pulled a few stones from her pocket. Lifting them up, she gestured to Cait.

"These? These are offerings. Never come on this beach without them," Fiona said sternly. She walked forward a few steps and drew a large circle in the sand with her big toe. Without looking, she motioned for Cait to join her inside the circle.

"What…" Cait began but Fiona cut her off quickly.

"Shh." Fiona sliced a glare at Cait and she shut up.

"To those that rest here, we offer these gifts as a token of our respect. In return we ask for your protection during our time here. Our purpose is pure." On those words Fiona tossed the flowers and the rocks into the water. Cait found herself trying to bite back a laugh but when the water slapped higher on the beach than usual, she clasped her mouth shut.

"This is very serious, Cait. You must never come here without first offering a gift and asking for protection. This is how people die. How you could die," Fiona said.

Cait shivered at the truth in the old woman's words.

"Come." Fiona motioned her forward and together they began to walk the beach. Fiona was silent for a while and Cait allowed herself to begin to relax. Truly, the cove was stunning. A private, mystical beach that was untouched in its beauty. The dogs ran the beach and dug in the sand, all but laughing their joy at being by the water.

"Do you know the history of Grace O'Malley?" Fiona asked.

"I do. It's hard to live in the town of Grace's Cove and not know about Grace O'Malley," Cait said with a shrug. The small village that they lived in had been named after Grace O'Malley, the famous pirate queen. She'd been ferocious on land and at sea, staunchly romantic, and Irish to the core. Her battles with the English had done much to preserve Celtic tradition. The most famous story surrounded her giving birth at sea mid-battle. But Cait knew that the most important story came not from how she lived her life, but how she had ended it.

"She's here, isn't she?" Cait nodded towards the water.

"Aye, she is," Fiona said. "She knew she was dying. Grace had a strong and pure intuition. She knew it was her time. Her daughter helped her to get down here and together they blessed and protected the cove. The night that Grace burned on the water is the same night that her daughter birthed her baby on the beach, alone."

Cait shuddered to think of it. How horrible to lose your mother and birth your child in one night…not to mention having to do it all on your own.

"Things were different back then," Fiona said, reading the thoughts on her face. "Women were more stoic. And it is through the powerful magick that transpired that night that the daughters of Grace all carry extra gifts. Her blood-line runs strong and there are more of you out there than you know."

"Well, sure, I mean, Ireland is such a mish-mash of family history. I'm sure we are all interconnected somehow."

"True, but not all carry the bloodline. It must go mother to daughter straight from Grace, not a male son who then births a daughter," Fiona explained.

"So…wait, does that mean my mother has a gift?" Cait exclaimed, and put her hand on Fiona's arm to stop her from continuing down the beach. Cait's cheeks flushed and she could swear that she heard a roaring in her head. All these years her mother and she had bickered, never really seeing eye to eye. They'd always been poor, and Cait's mother had often disapproved of Cait's decision to open a pub and try to better herself. "We're simple people, Cait

Gallagher," was her mother's constant refrain. Not so simple, after all, it seemed, Cait thought.

Fiona said nothing, simply waiting for Cait to put the dots together.

"Well, of course she does. So if every daughter of Grace has something, then what is hers?"

Fiona turned to her and smiled gently.

"That would be a conversation you're to be having with your mother, not me, lass." Fiona pulled a worn tartan blanket from her bag and bent to spread it on the sand. Cait caught the rough corners of the blanket and helped Fiona to stretch it out. Fiona plopped down and patted the spot next to her and Cait joined her, the sand lumpy beneath her bottom.

Ronan rushed over and jumped on Cait, giving her one rough swipe with his tongue before turning to tear off across the beach. Cait choked out a laugh and wiped his slobber from her face with the back of her arm.

"Interesting, isn't it, how much animals love you?" Fiona asked.

Cait felt a small nerve of awkwardness twinge in her but instead of immediately contradicting Fiona, she took a deep breath.

"I...I can read their thoughts too," Cait admitted carefully, keeping her eyes trained on the water that kissed the rocks of the cliff. She was worried that Fiona would think she was weird.

"I suspected as much. What a marvelous gift!" Fiona's excitement rang pure and true and Cait felt her heart fill with light.

"Really? You don't think it is weird? I mean…people, yeah, but animals?"

"Why should the ability to read thoughts be constrained to just humans? We aren't the only species capable of thinking," Fiona said excitedly.

"So is that what you wanted to work with me on? Being a pet whisperer or something?" Cait asked.

"No, though I think the idea is wonderful." Fiona laughed at her. "Perhaps you should have been a vet."

"I probably would have if I could have afforded the education. Far too rich for my blood," Cait said.

"Well, we all have our paths. You never know where yours will take you. However, I want to talk to you about how you currently use your ability," Fiona said.

"I don't. I mean, not really. Once in a while I will catch a stray thought or I will let my shields down to scan someone's thoughts but for the most part, I don't. I…I feel like it is wrong so I stuff it way down inside of me," Cait admitted softly. She looked down at her hands to find them clenched tightly in her lap.

"Ah, yes, you've always held yourself to a very exacting code of honor, haven't you?"

Cait shrugged one shoulder and nodded.

"It just doesn't seem right…peeking in on people's thoughts. I have lived so long shielding myself that now I rarely do it. Though it is fun to do with dogs. They are just so happy."

"Ronan," Fiona called and Ronan raced to them. "Will he understand if I ask him a question?"

"I…I don't really know. I haven't had full conversations before, I just catch snatches of commentary," Cait said.

"Well, let's see what happens," Fiona said. She turned to Ronan and invited him to lie down on the blanket before her. Teagan sat behind him.

"Ronan, do you like living at the cottage?"

Cait lowered her shields and reached out to Ronan. His thoughts came to her through a pink haze of love and happiness.

"Love house. Love you. Love Mom."

"He says that he loves the house and loves you and Keelin," Cait said.

"Do you want to stay at Keelin and Flynn's or at the cottage?" Fiona asked, raising the complexity level of the question.

"Cottage. Love cottage. Friend. You need friend."

Cait stared at the dog, her mouth hanging open. She had no idea why she hadn't tried this before and was quite certain that she would never look at an animal the same again.

"Um, gosh, he said that he wants to live with you because you need a friend."

Fiona's face softened and she rubbed Ronan's head.

"Don't feel like you have to stay, buddy. I have lots of friends."

"No. Stay." The dog pushed his head into Fiona's hand.

"Well, I guess you are going to have to break the bad news to Keelin that Ronan is staying with you," Cait said with a chuckle.

Fiona laughed.

"Okay, Ronan, if you stay where will you sleep and what's your favorite meal?" Fiona said inquisitively.

"On your bed. Bed. Foot of bed. All the meals. Love meals. Food. Food. Food."

Cait couldn't help but chuckle at the dog's enthusiastic response.

"It appears that he will be sleeping at the foot of your bed and he seems fairly easy to please on the food front. He likes it all."

Fiona laughed and leaned over to wrap her arms around Ronan.

"Okay, buddy. You get to stay with me. We'll deal with Keelin. Now, go play."

Cait shook her head and couldn't help but feel like her whole body was lit with joy. She'd had her first real conversation with an animal. It was fascinating and provocative and, quite simply, beautiful.

"I…I, just wow. I'm amazed at this."

"It's a beautiful thing, isn't it? Power?" Fiona leaned back on her hands and gazed at the water.

"So, you said that you have lessons for me. What did you mean?"

"Not lessons so much as an uncovering. I think that it is time for you to start using your gift more. For the greater good," Fiona said.

"What? How could I do that?"

"Fairly easily if you put your mind to it," Fiona said quietly.

Cait stared at the edge of the water where it blurred into the horizon. How could she use it for the greater good? She'd never considered her gift as something that could be useful, instead it had always been something that she had tried to hide or ignore. A guilty feeling crept up on her as she thought about how many nights Fiona dedicated to healing others. And now that Keelin had embraced her power to heal with her hands, she also joined Fiona quite frequently in her healing sessions. Cait had been so engrossed in getting the pub up and running that she'd done little to help others at all as of late.

"I suppose that I should do more to lend a hand. Can I help you with your healings?" Cait asked.

Fiona tilted her head at Cait. "I don't know, can you?"

Cait thought about it.

"I suppose if someone is unable to talk then I'd be able to help in that respect?"

A quick smile shot across Fiona's face.

"You absolutely could. But you understand what you would be opening yourself up to, right?"

Cait shook her head no.

"Well, say you connected mentally with someone unable to speak. If their family is in the room then they are going to know about your gift. Healing is one of those things where you either embrace it fully or you stay hidden. Or, you find other ways to use your ability."

"I hadn't thought about it like that. How do you deal with it? With people knowing that you are different?"

"Well, to be honest, I don't really deal with it at all. I just let myself be me and other people are forced to wrap their heads around it. For those that I have healed from the brink of death or serious sickness…they don't even bother trying to understand. They are simply grateful. Others, well, they don't want to understand so they don't associate with me. But, with anything, if someone doesn't want to know the real me then I don't need them in my life, you understand?"

Cait nodded. It made sense and yet...

"God, I've lived with this secret for so long. I don't know how people in the village would react."

"Do you really think that nobody else in this village has secrets?" Fiona raised an eyebrow at her.

"I guess that I hadn't really thought about it like that. I don't know. I'm scared," Cait admitted and shrugged her shoulders. Her stomach twisted in knots at the thought of revealing her ability to people.

"Fear is a useless emotion," Fiona said forcefully.

"I...okay, yes, I get that." Cait blew out a sigh and watched the dogs race through the waves, barking at each other.

"Mrs. Donovan, the older one, recently had a stroke. She lost her ability to speak and her hands are too shaky to write. She might appreciate some company," Fiona suggested.

Cait looked down at her hands, clenched so tightly in her lap. *Okay*, she thought, *an old woman needs help. I can do this*. Coming to a resolution in her mind, she turned to Fiona.

"I'll go to see her this afternoon."

CHAPTER 7

*C*AIT THOUGHT ABOUT what Fiona had said on her drive back into Grace's Cove. She'd lived with hiding her gift for so long that it felt weird to consider using it in a different capacity.

They say the early teenage years are the most awkward for children and Cait's hadn't been any different, she thought. The ability to read people's minds had just about sent Cait screaming for the hills. It was like she had a front-row seat to every crush, break-up, and fight that her friends at school were involved in. As if being a teenager wasn't difficult enough, having to try and act normal when she could read what people were thinking about her had caused Cait more than her fair share of problems.

Cait thought of her mother and shook her head. The few times she had tried to approach Sarah about what was going on, her mother had made the sign of the cross and had started whispering "Hail Marys" as she rocked her chair in front of her favorite TV shows.

Cait's relationship with her mother was a complicated

one. Growing up in Ireland meant that family came first. But, because her only family was a mother that barely acknowledged her, it had really felt like Cait was raising herself.

Sarah rarely made time for Cait. What with her mother working double shifts at the market and catching up on her favorite television shows, Cait had usually eaten her dinners alone, often not speaking with her mother for days at a time. By the time Cait was fifteen, they saw each other as infrequently as possible. The times they did speak generally erupted into bitter feuds.

It had soon become known around Grace's Cove that Cait was at a loss for familial support. Gradually, the invitations to dinner at her friends' houses increased and the families of Grace's Cove shifted to include her as one of their own. Cait's roots were entwined as much with the families of this town as they were with the blood that ran in the cove.

Cait thought back to those awkward, agonizing years. She almost saw those years through a lens of burning shame. Shame that she couldn't understand why she could hear people's thoughts. Shame from having a mother that wanted little to do with her. And, guilt at not being good enough for her mother. Cait excelled in school and had constantly tried to talk to her mother about her aspirations after school. She was met with a cold wall of silence.

Until Fiona.

Fiona had all but plucked Cait from the streets of Grace's Cove and spent the weekends putting her to work around her house. Slowly, as they had built a relationship, Cait had opened up to Fiona. It had only taken a few shaky conversations before Fiona had told Cait what she was, and in doing so, pulled Cait back from the brink and saved her from losing herself.

Once Fiona had taught Cait to shield herself from others' thoughts, Cait had been able to walk easily among the other students. She dated, made new friends, lost friends, and did all the normal things that a teenage girl did.

Though, there were those few times. Cait laughed up at herself in the rearview mirror. Once she'd gotten used to her ability, she'd had a few moments where she used it to get the upper hand in a situation. She still remembered the horrified look on one teacher's face when she tried to force the whole class to stay after school for being rowdy until Cait had cornered the teacher and threatened to tell everyone about her crush on the local doctor. The class had gotten to go home and the teacher had stayed far away from Cait after that.

Cait had moved out of her mother's apartment as soon as school was finished. She'd worked two jobs to make the rent, but her freedom had been priceless. Her relationship with her mother had deteriorated even further. Yet, a part of Cait still hoped for something more. She dutifully brought her mother food each week and tried to stop by for tea as her schedule permitted. The visits were usually short.

And then. That day. The day her future had become glaringly clear to her.

Cait pictured the For Lease sign on the front of Murphy's Pub. It had been the talk of the town as Murphy's

Pub had held the title of longest-running pub in Grace's Cove.

Cait could see her hands trembling as she gripped the folder of papers for her business loan documents from the bank. It had seemed like forever as the banker had pored over each and every detail of her documents. Finally, he had looked up and smiled at her.

"This is an excellent business plan. I agree, adding a kitchen and food will do well for the pub. I look forward to you serving me your first pint," he'd said, and laughed as Cait jumped up and ran around the desk to hug him. Finally, something of her own.

From that day on, she'd never looked back. She ate, slept, and breathed the pub and shielding her ability had become even more important. Though, Cait found that most people would end up telling their secrets after a few pints anyway, but she still did her best not to let her ability impact what she was creating for herself.

Cait smiled as she thought about the little nest egg that she'd been slowly building over the last three years. In a few years, she'd own the pub outright if she could convince the owner to sell it.

And her mother? Well, she'd just have to accept that this was what Cait wanted to do with her life. Though Cait held little hope that Sarah would come to see her side of things, she still tried.

Releasing a long breath, Cait drove her car into downtown and pushed thoughts of the past out of her head. Today would be a new way to use her gift and hopefully it would make up for the ways she had used it in the past.

CHAPTER 8

*C*AIT PULLED HER car up in front of the bright blue building that housed the little flower shop in town. She figured that Mrs. Donovan might like some flowers. And, Cait knew that she was stalling. What if the Donovans were scared of her? Or told the village everything about her? Her stomach was twisted in knots and a dull sense of worry pulsed through her.

Cait took a deep breath to calm herself. The Donovans needed her help. Surely, kindness wouldn't backfire on her. Cait stepped from her car and walked to the door, jumping back as it swung open.

Shane stepped out, his arms full of Gerbera daisies, one of her favorite flowers. Instant jealously blinded Cait to the way his face lit when he saw her on the sidewalk.

"For your girlfriend, I suppose?" Cait sneered at Shane. He stopped dead in his tracks and stiffened. Cait immediately felt bad as the smile dropped from his face. Shane just shook his head at her.

"Well...go on. Don't want to keep blonde, tall, and gorgeous waiting, do you?"

"What's your problem, Cait?" Shane asked directly.

"Mine? What's yours? Did your girl catch you kissing me? Those flowers for an apology?" Cait raised an eyebrow at him and crossed her arms over her chest.

"Actually, they were for you. But damned if I'll be giving them up now," Shane said, and turned from her, striding angrily across the street to his car.

Cait's mouth dropped open and she tried to think of a single thing to say but nothing came out. The slow heat of shame slipped up her cheeks and she dropped her head before pulling the door open to step into the cool shop. Shane was going to bring her flowers? And her favorite ones at that? She couldn't help but feel a trickle of warmth go through her. How did he even know what her favorite flowers were, she wondered.

"Hullo there, Cait," Anne, the owner of the flower shop, called out to her.

"Hi, Anne," Cait said and moved into the shop, allowing the pretty scents and cool air to wash over her.

"What brings you in today?"

"I heard that Mrs. Donovan had a stroke. I thought that I might stop by, bring her something pretty," Cait said.

"Aye, that's right nice of you, Cait. Her favorites are lilies and I have some lovely ones in today." Anne gestured to the case where a variety of lilies stood in tall buckets.

"Let's do a mix of colors, a happy bunch," Cait decided.

"Yes, ma'am," Anne said. Cait half listened as she chattered about Keelin's wedding. Her brain was whirling with thoughts of why Shane would be bringing her flowers. Was he really dating the blonde? Did he feel bad about kissing Cait the other night? If Shane lived by his own code of honor then he probably felt bad because he was her landlord, Cait thought stubbornly. Frustrated, she paced in front of the buckets of flowers.

"All set, Cait. Tell her that I send my love," Anne said cheerfully and Cait grabbed the wrapped bunch of flowers and left to begin the drive along the coast.

CHAPTER 9

*S*HANE SAT IN his car and stared at the bouquet of flowers on the front seat. What had he been thinking…bringing Cait flowers? That woman was more stubborn than the old mule he kept housed out at his stables. Shane blew out a breath and slammed his fist onto the steering wheel.

He'd loved Cait Gallagher for a while now. Though they'd gone to school together, she was younger than him and had never come onto his radar until that one day.

That day…Shane closed his eyes and thought back to the day when Cait had burned her path straight into his mind and down into his heart.

He'd been at the market, picking up his usual bachelor fare for dinner, and had heard hushed voices arguing. Tilting his head, Shane had peered around a stack of produce to see Cait arguing with her mother, who worked at the market.

"You'll fail, just like the Gallaghers have always failed," Sarah had hissed at Cait.

Cait had stood before her mother, her chin held high, fire burning in her eyes.

"I won't fail," Cait said.

"You're stupid to think that you can run a pub," Sarah said.

"I'm not. It's a good business plan. The bank agrees," Cait said adamantly.

"Borrowing money to go into debt...only to fail. You'll only do worse for yourself. I, for one, won't support this foolish idea of yours," Sarah said and crossed her arms, looking down her nose at her daughter.

"I want something more for myself, Ma, can't you see that?" Cait had whispered and Shane had wanted to rush in and protect her from Sarah. He'd seen the business plan when Cait had approached him about renting his property. It was just what the pub needed to breathe new life into the downtown area and Shane was quite certain it would be a smashing success. But, he knew better than to involve himself in a family fight.

Shane had watched as Cait continued to defend herself against her mother before Sarah threw up her hands and walked away. Shane had watched Cait's face fall and the sheen of tears enter her eyes. He'd wanted nothing more than to reassure her that he would make sure that she never failed but something had stopped him. Cait had taken a deep breath and wiped her eyes before sailing from the store. She had never looked more beautiful than in her moment of fierceness and Shane had found his interest piqued.

Over the past three years, Shane had watched Cait put her heart and soul into Gallagher's pub. She'd grown it into a thriving business that was the hub of the community. Sarah still refused to step foot in the door but Shane imagined that Cait was probably okay with that.

Shane often found himself daydreaming about Cait. About the way her hair curled over her smooth cheeks or how her pretty green eyes lit with laughter at a joke that one of her patrons would tell her. She exuded a quiet confidence in a pint-sized package. A package that he had longed to undress for years.

Shane groaned as he thought about the kiss from the other night. Two kisses he'd had now. Her taste was burned into his mind, forever changing how he would look at Cait. He'd tried to quash his feelings for her for a while now. As her landlord, dating her would be unethical, Shane thought. But...her lips. The kiss by the cove felt like it had been the kiss to end all kisses for him. From now on, there would be no other. He'd been stupid to bring Ellen to the wedding with him. There was no point to making Cait jealous, Shane thought.

With a frustrated sigh, Shane started his car and drove towards the pub. Though she didn't necessarily deserve flowers after the way she'd treated him, it was time to keep Cait Gallagher on her toes, Shane thought with a smile.

CHAPTER 10

T HE DONOVANS LIVED a ways out of the village along a small road that led to low cliffs overlooking the sparkling water. It was a lovely spot, though it had to be difficult for an invalid to live in now, Cait thought. She wondered how Mrs. Donovan's husband was coping.

Cait turned on a small curve in the road and pulled into the gravel drive that led to a gray stone cottage with a thatched roof. Mr. Donovan was working in the yard. A rotund man, he had on farmer's overalls and a straw hat. He straightened at the sound of a car and lifted an arm in a wave to Cait. Cait turned the car off and, grabbing the flowers, crossed the front lawn to greet him.

"Mr. Donovan, good to see you," Cait called.

"Aye, Cait, good to see you too. I hope this isn't about my tab at the pub," he said cheerfully.

Cait laughed at him and reached up to kiss his cheek.

"No, I've come to see the missus. I heard about her stroke," Cait said.

The light went out of his eyes and he nodded sadly. "It's sad. Hard to see her like this. I wish that I could do more for her." Mr. Donovan shrugged his shoulders helplessly.

"Well, maybe I can help with that. Can I talk to her?"

"Sure you can, but she can't really answer back more than a shake of her head," Mr. Donovan said. He led her around the house to where a cluster of trees stood. The view of the sea was unobstructed here and Mrs. Donovan sat beneath the trees in the shade they provided. Her eyes followed them as they walked closer.

"Hi, Mrs. Donovan, I brought you flowers," Cait said. She held them out awkwardly before realizing that Mrs. Donovan wouldn't be able to reach for them.

"Here, I'll just show you all the different colors," Cait said and turned the bouquet so Mrs. Donovan could admire them. Letting down her shields, Cait scanned the old woman's brain.

"I love lilies. Oh, they are so precious. They would be perfect in my crystal vase from our wedding."

Cait handed them to Mr. Donovan.

"Um, do you maybe have a pretty crystal vase for these?"

"We sure do. A lovely one from our wedding. I'll find it now." Mr. Donovan pulled another chair close for Cait and then crossed the grass to go inside.

Cait blew out a breath and sat in the chair, taking Mrs. Donovan's hand in hers. It was now or never, she thought. She cleared her throat awkwardly a few times.

"Okay, so…ahem, this is going to sound weird, but just

hear me out," Cait stammered. "Gosh, I don't really know how to say this."

Cait turned to see the old woman's eyes tracking her avidly.

"I, um, well, it's like this: I can read minds," Cait rushed out in a breath. Mrs. Donovan's eyebrow rose.

"So, I just thought, maybe you'd like to talk to me a bit. I can hear you if you'd like. So, do you want me to try?"

Mrs. Donovan stared at her for a moment and then gave a subtle nod, yes, with her head.

Cait let down her shields and listened.

"Can you really hear me? I feel like I'm dead in here but my mind has so many thoughts. I'm still here."

"Of course you're still here. You're still a person. We know that," Cait said automatically and then gasped as Mrs. Donovan choked and a slow trickle of tears poured from her eyes.

"Oh, no, please don't cry, Mr. Donovan will kick me out," Cait said desperately.

"I...I'm just so happy to talk to someone," Mrs. Donovan thought.

"I know and I'm sorry that I didn't come sooner. I...I just...not many people know about this," Cait said.

"Well, your secret is safe with me," Mrs. Donovan said in her mind and winked at her and Cait burst out laughing.

"Well, it looks like you two are having fun," Mr. Donovan boomed across the yard. He hurried over to see the tears on his wife's cheeks. Instantly he straightened to glare at Cait. "Why is she crying?"

"Tell him. He doesn't gossip. Tell him, please. Oh, I so want to talk to him again," Mrs. Donovan instructed Cait.

"Um, well, so, it's like this…" Cait stammered. "I, uh, can kind of read minds."

Mr. Donovan's face went a little white and he turned to gape at his wife.

"What? You can talk to her?" Mr. Donovan gestured to his wife.

"Yes, sir, I can."

"Tell me what color underwear I put on this morning," Mr. Donovan demanded.

"He put the faded blue ones on that I've told him to get rid of a million times," Mrs. Donovan said. Cait quirked a smile at her.

"Um, your old blue ones that she told you to get rid of a million times."

Mr. Donovan gasped and, bending over, he scooped Cait from her chair and twirled her in a circle before putting her down to kiss his wife tenderly.

"Tell him that he's been making the bread wrong," Mrs. Donovan said.

"You've been making the bread wrong," Cait said.

"Don't I know it? Thank God you've come." Mr. Donovan chuckled and, drawing up a chair, he began to pepper his wife with questions. Cait laughed and soon fell into an easy rhythm of conversation for an hour. As the sun slipped towards the horizon, Mr. Donovan stood.

"I'll need to help her to the bathroom and start dinner. You're welcome to stay, of course," he said eagerly.

"I have to go, I'm sorry."

Mr. Donovan held her hand and stared into her eyes.

"You've given us a great gift today. I don't know how to ask this but I'd be willing to pay you or help with chores at the pub or anything you need if you could see it in your heart to stop by here and there. Just...so we can talk." Mr. Donovan gulped and Cait felt her heart tear a bit for the couple.

"I'll make this my Monday afternoon stop, okay? Save up your questions for Mondays. And, in the meantime, maybe we can start devising a system of signals for the both of you to communicate. Think about it this week," Cait suggested. She leaned over to kiss Mrs. Donovan's cheek.

"Bless you, Cait. A thousand blessings. You've given me my voice back. I'm forever beholden to you," Mrs. Donovan said.

"No, really, it's nothing. The least that I can do," Cait said, embarrassed.

She left the couple smiling happily at each other. Cait felt a sense of lightness fill her on the drive home. It was a new feeling, one that came from truly helping someone else. She thought that maybe Fiona had been right after all about claiming her power. It wasn't all about her, there was so much more that she could do with her ability. She'd spent her whole life hiding it when she could have been helping others. A pang of sadness hit her as she thought about the old couple and their love for each other. She wanted that...that true, pure love.

Detouring past the pub, she parked her car and stopped in to pick up the mail. Cait gasped as she stepped into the dim interior and saw a large vase of Gerbera daisies on the bar.

"Those were dropped off for you...there's a note," her chef called before passing back into the kitchen.

Trying to keep a smile from her lips, Cait crossed to the bar and plucked the note from among the blooms. She opened it and read the one word it held.

Stupid.

Cait huffed out a laugh at the same time she felt anger fill her. How did he do it? Make her mad and make her laugh at the same time? Cait nibbled at her lip as she looked at the cheerful bunch of flowers. She felt like things were shifting, yet she couldn't seem to get her feet on solid ground with Shane. Frustrated, Cait whisked the vase from the bar and left for her tiny apartment.

CHAPTER 11

C
AIT WAITED ANXIOUSLY for her coffee to brew. She'd barely slept the night before and when she had, her dreams had been filled with images of Shane with the blonde. Which was stupid, Cait thought. She didn't even know what their relationship was. It wasn't like he was bringing the blonde flowers. Or was he? Cait thought about it but just couldn't wrap her head around Shane going after two women. And yet... Trying to push her insecurities aside, Cait pulled out a coffee cup and thought about her trip to see the Donovans yesterday.

She was filled with a strange mixture of excitement over discovering how her gift could help others and nervousness about what this would mean for her future. If she continued to help others, would the word get out? Would there be people lining up at her door trying to use her as a lie detector in their business dealings? Cait could only imagine the nefarious ways that people would try to take advantage of her. Which was why she'd always hidden her gift, Cait thought.

She went back to thinking about Shane and the blonde dancing at the wedding.

"Sure and he can take every other woman in Ireland out on a date but me," Cait said grumpily. The scent of coffee teased her nose and she breathed a sigh of relief as the pot finished brewing. Pouring a cup, she took it with her to the shower. Since she was up so early, Cait wanted to stop by her mother's for a word.

She tried not to let her thoughts stray to Shane during her shower. It was hard not to as the bouquet of flowers was a constant reminder of him. She had placed them by her bed last night and foolishly smiled at the cheerful blossoms each time she looked at them. Cait rinsed her hair and tried to focus on other things. She was dangerously afraid that she was becoming besotted with Shane. Instead, she needed to think about how she would approach her mother.

Sarah Gallagher worked as a cashier at the local food market. She had never traveled out of Grace's Cove, had raised Cait by herself after Cait's father had left when Cait was just a baby, and feared anything that she didn't understand. Sarah's whole world was her job and her TV shows. Cait had always confused Sarah with her need to make something of herself and her business. Cait bit her lip as the old resentment crept in while she towel dried her hair. Until she settled down with a man and did "woman's work" her mother would never approve of her. Cait sniffed. It hurt her heart, just a bit, to know that Sarah and she would never have a friendship.

Cait wondered why her mother had never told her that she had her own special gifts. Did her mother just deny it or did she refuse to talk about it? Cait wondered how Sarah would react when Cait confronted her about it. Maybe, just maybe, this would be the link that finally drew them closer. It would be nice to find something to connect with her mother about.

Mulling over these thoughts, Cait slipped into her uniform of jeans and a stretchy tank top. Usually she flew out of her apartment with wet hair and little to no makeup. An image of Shane's beautiful blonde flashed through her head and with a groan, Cait walked back to her vanity and examined herself in the mirror. The deep purple of her tank was a flattering color for her eyes and skin tone. Cait picked up a pretty beaded necklace that Aislinn had made for her and slipped it over her neck, allowing it to drape over her chest and to dress up her casual outfit. She pumped some mousse into her hands and wound it through her tousled mop of curls, smoothing their wildness. Cait squinted and then with a sigh, added just a hint of eyeliner and some blush for a nice punch of color to her face. Slamming the eye pencil down, Cait decided that was enough, grabbed her messenger bag and left her tiny apartment.

Pounding down the stairs, Cait skidded to a stop to press a kiss to Mr. O'Leary's papery cheek as he gathered his mail by the door.

"You're a good girl, Cait." Mr. O'Leary smiled and waved her on.

Cait smiled and stepped out onto the street, breathing in the morning air that carried a hint of the sea with it. Though she yearned to travel more, Cait had never been one to take for granted the beauty of their tiny village tucked in the hills by the sea. She whistled as she passed the brightly colored buildings that made up the main street and were quintessentially Irish in design. Hodgepodge stores nestled next to the bank and the chemist, each building painted a different color, windows lined with lace curtains and ringed with boxes full of flowers. Cait waved a hand at the banker as she passed his window and turned up the hill to make her way to her mother's tiny apartment building. She knew that Tuesdays were Sarah's afternoon shift so Cait would be able to catch her mother for an early cup of tea.

Cait reached the small white stucco building that housed four miniscule apartments. Though she had a key, she pressed the buzzer to her mother's apartment. They didn't have the "drop in unannounced" type of relationship.

"Yes?"

"Ma, it's me."

The door clicked open and Cait took the smooth wood stairs two at a time before reaching her mother's apartment on the second floor. The door stood open and Cait stepped through into her childhood home, the scent of lemon polish and freshly baked bread enveloping her. A small dining-room table dominated the room. To the right, a low brown couch and recliner lined a wall with windows. A small television sat directly across from the recliner. Cait had spent most of her life sleeping on that lumpy couch. A morose kitchenette with a paned window over the sink completed the main room. A tiny hallway led to her mother's room and a bathroom. As usual, the apartment was immaculate and the television was blaring with the morning talk shows. Sarah stood at the stove with a teapot.

"Tea?"

"Sure, I'll have a cup," Cait said and moved to sit down at the table. It would be useless to help her mother, as Sarah never liked people to do things for her. Sarah brought Cait her tea with just a dash of milk and lemon, the way that Cait loved it. Cait's stomach did a little flip as she thought about how to approach the conversation she wanted to have.

"What brings you here today?" Sarah asked.

"Can't I just stop by to see you?" Cait asked.

"Well, yes, you certainly can, Cait. No need to be rude," Sarah said huffily and eased her thin frame into the chair across from Cait.

Cait studied her mother's face, so much like her own. Deep worry lines etched Sarah's forehead and her shoulders slumped forward, giving her a constantly defeated look. Cait wondered if Sarah had been different before Cait's father had left.

"I'm sorry, I didn't sleep well," Cait said and blew on her tea. Sarah didn't say anything and Cait gave her a small smile. It had always been like this between them. Forced conversations, awkward hugs, and a lot of underlying resentment.

"I...well, I wanted to talk to you about something kind of important," Cait began.

"Oh? Finally giving up on that foolish pub dream of yours?" Sarah asked as she calmly stirred her tea.

Cait felt her breath hitch and she closed her eyes for a moment, gathering her calm. Now was not the time to go over all of the reasons that the pub was the best thing for her. Cait had long since stopped defending her choices to her mother.

"No, actually the pub is doing great and I am making a profit, thanks for asking though," Cait said bitterly. "I have something else to talk about."

Sarah gestured with her mug for Cait to continue.

"Do you have any special abilities that you haven't told me about?"

Cait quickly dropped her shields and reached out to her mother's mind as Sarah carefully composed her face.

"I don't really understand what you mean. Are you looking to hire me or something?" Sarah said deliberately.

Cait shook her head and listened to her mother's mind. Getting what she needed, she put her shields back up and calmly met her mother's eyes.

"You're lying."

"I most certainly am not. What are you talking about? This is confusing, Cait. I don't have time for this, my show is on." Sarah shot a glance to the small television.

Thinking quickly, Cait pulled a Gerbera daisy from her purse that she had foolishly tucked into the outside pocket earlier today. She slid it across the table to her mother.

"Who gave this to me?"

An angry look crossed Sarah's face and she kept her hands on the teacup.

"I have no idea, I'm quite certain one of the foolish lads that sniff around you at the pub," Sarah said and lifted her chin at Cait.

"You could though…couldn't you? If you wanted? You'd be able to touch that flower and tell me who it was from," Cait said stubbornly.

"That's ridiculous."

"Is it?"

Cait met her mother's eyes and held them. She jumped as Sarah stood up and threw her teacup across the room, the cup shattering against the wall. Cait leapt out of her chair and turned between the broken remnants of the cup and her mother. Sarah's hands were trembling and her chest was heaving with emotion.

"Get out. Don't come back," Sarah said, her voice low with menace.

"What? Mother, you can't mean that!" Cait said, astounded at the response.

"This is the devil's work. I knew that you were tainted. As am I. I did something wrong…somewhere along the line. This is my cross to bear," Sarah said quietly. She walked to the kitchen to get a broom, muttering about God and the devil. Cait's body trembled with fear for her mother. It wasn't until now that she realized that her mom had moved past reclusive into crazy.

"Mom, these are gifts. Not the devil's work. You can use it to help others," Cait said gently. She moved towards her mom and Sarah held up the broom in front of her small body.

"Stay away from me, Cait Gallagher. I no longer acknowledge you as my daughter," Sarah said.

"Ma, stop. You are being way too dramatic. Can't we work through this?"

Sarah raised her eyes to meet Cait's. The older woman trembled with emotion and for a moment, her eyes looked through Cait.

"No, I don't suppose that we can. We've always been too different. I don't want what you want. I'm happy with the way my life is. You have delusions of grandeur with trying to be some fancy pub owner. And, if you think that a poor girl like you is going to fit into rich Shane MacAuliffe's life...you're dead wrong. Yes, I know that is who gave you the flower just as I know that he is far too rich for your blood. You'd be smart to settle down with a fisherman or a farmer, make babies, and stop trying to rock the boat. Now, get out."

Cait's heart cracked a bit and her eyes blurred with tears. She'd thought she was past the pain that her mother could inflict on her but it seemed that no matter what, she'd always want that approval. With a small nod, Cait turned her back to her mother and slammed the door, running blindly into the street.

She couldn't go to work like this, Cait thought and turning, she ran up the street, away from the town, away from it all.

A late-model sedan slowed by her side.

"You alright there, Cait?"

Shit, shit, shit...was all Cait could think. She would know Shane's voice anywhere. Refusing to look at the car, she continued to walk on the side of the road, hoping he would go away. She sighed as she heard the car stop and the door close.

"Cait, wait," Shane said from behind her.

Cait continued to pound her feet on the pavement and willed herself to stop crying. She stiffened as Shane grabbed her arm and forced her to stop. Cait swallowed and turning, she met his eyes. Instant concern flashed across his handsome face.

"Oh, what's wrong? Are you hurt?" Instantly, Shane

ran his hands over her arms, down her waist and over her legs. "Where does it hurt?"

Cait froze as heat trailed down her body wherever his hands touched. A warm ripple of lust tugged low in her stomach.

"I'm not hurt. Just, it's nothing," Cait said.

Shane surprised her and pulled her close for a hug. Cait held her back ramrod straight and struggled to breathe.

"It's okay to lean on someone, you know," Shane whispered. Cait nodded against his hard chest and giving in a little, allowed herself to melt into his hug.

"There you are. Now tell me who I have to beat up," Shane said.

Cait hiccupped out a laugh and stepped back, wiping away her tears.

"Unless you are into beating up old women, I don't think that there is much that you can do," Cait said.

"Your mom again?" Shane asked. He'd watched more than his fair share of Cait and Sarah's battles throughout the years after Cait had opened the pub.

"Aye, though this one was a bad one. I don't suspect we will be seeing much of each other after this."

"No, but she's your mother!" Shane said.

"I know. I...I'm not sure if she is right in her head to be honest. She's always been reclusive but today she kicked me out and ended our relationship," Cait admitted.

Shane stared at her, his mouth hanging open in disbelief.

"Well, that's completely un-Irish," Shane said and teased a laugh from Cait.

"Isn't it just? Ah, well, we've never been your normal

Irish family, as you know. I've got Fiona and my friends.
I'll be fine." Cait shrugged her shoulders helplessly.

"And me," Shane said softly, his hands still on her
shoulders.

Cait nodded softly and lost herself for a moment in his
warm brown eyes. Shane glanced around quickly at the
street. Finding it empty, he leaned over and brushed the
softest of kisses across Cait's tear-stained lips. For some
reason, this gentle gesture made tears well up in her eyes
again.

"No, no, God, no, please don't cry more. Shit, that is
the last thing a man wants is a woman to cry at his kiss,"
Shane said and awkwardly patted her arms.

A swell of laughter bubbled up through Cait and
escaped in a choked gurgle. Too many emotions swarmed
through her and, bending over at the waist, she laughed
from her gut, unable to stop. Catching her breath, she
stood to find Shane with his hands on his waist, a grumpy
look on his face.

"Well, I'm glad to see that I was able to cheer you up,"
Shane said.

"Oh God, I'm sorry, it's just…too much," Cait gasped.
Shane nodded and started to turn, hurt in his eyes.

Acting on impulse, Cait wrapped her arms around his
neck, pulling his face down to meet hers. She pressed her
lips to his blindly and prayed that he wouldn't reject her.
Shane's arms wrapped around her waist and drew her
closer. Cait let out a small sigh and moaned slightly as
Shane deepened the kiss, nibbling lightly at her lower lip.
Heat shot straight through her core.

A cheerful horn honk startled them apart and Shane

waved as a blue van drove past. Cait kept her face averted but she could feel the color creep up her cheeks.

"Well, now, this will be some gossip for the town," Shane said cheerfully. He stepped back and gestured to his car. "Need a ride?"

Unable to speak, Cait nodded. She had no idea where to take this from here.

"Off to open the pub?"

Again, Cait nodded. She stayed silent on the drive to the pub and nodded a few times at Shane's cheerful discussion of the weather and some local gossip. Pulling up to the pub, Cait turned to thank him quickly, meaning to slip hastily from the car.

"Oh no you don't," Shane said and grabbed the strap of her purse, pulling her close for a blistering kiss. Cait gasped into his mouth and closed her eyes with a soft moan. Her body trembled and her mind emptied of thoughts. She jerked as Shane broke the kiss. Cait raised her hands to her lips; they felt like they were on fire. Shane raised an eyebrow at her and gave her a cocky smile before reaching across her and opening the door for her. Cait had never seen this side of Shane before. Deep down, she thought that she kind of liked it.

"Have a nice day, Cait," Shane said quietly and Cait nodded, unable to speak, and ran for the safety of the pub. Her stomach churned and her face flamed as his long, low chuckle floated from the window of his car.

CHAPTER 12

*C*AIT'S MOOD STAYED with her much of the day. After the second time she was short with a customer, she called Patrick over.

"Listen, Patrick, can you handle this? It should be fairly slow as we have no music tonight."

"Sure thing. Got a big date?" Patrick asked and Cait whipped her head around to scan his face.

"No. What makes you think that?" Cait said, menace lacing her tone.

"No reason. I was just joking," Patrick said, his hands in the air. Cait rolled her eyes. She really needed to calm down.

"Sorry, I'm just in a mood. Going to call it a night," Cait said.

"Okay, I'll call your cell phone if I need anything." Patrick smiled easily at her and Cait blew out a breath. She really needed a break or something…else. Cait was feeling itchy. As she walked home, Cait thought about how long it had been since she had dated anyone. Counting back…she realized it had been since before she opened the pub that she had dated. Why, that made almost three years! Cait stopped in her tracks at the realization that she had gone that long without sex. No wonder she was on edge, Cait thought. Her whole life had been devoted to the pub.

Cait arrived at her apartment and stood looking at the door. She didn't know what to do with herself. Not used to downtime, Cait typically didn't relax well. She eyed Aislinn's shop down the street and debated going to see her cousin. Aislinn would be able to see her emotional turmoil from a mile away, Cait thought. She wasn't quite ready to hash through everything that had happened today. Maybe she should take a drive out to see Fiona, instead.

Having made her decision, Cait detoured around her apartment building towards her bright red compact car in the back parking lot. A nice drive along the coast as the sun set would be a good way to unwind.

Cait rolled her windows down to encourage the sea breezes and turning her car towards the long seaside road, instead of the shorter route over the hills, she allowed the tension to drain out of her shoulders. Turning up the radio, Cait sang along to bad 90s music as she wound through the curves that hugged the cliffs. The sun was tipping towards the horizon and the water looked like someone had dropped a bag of diamonds onto a blanket of blue velvet. Cait felt her heart soar at the sight. She loved this cliff drive and doubted that she would ever tire of looking out over the water. There was something so incredibly soothing about the sea for her. Even when she was younger, if she had a fight with her mom, she'd bike to the water and stay there for hours, allowing the magnetic pull of the ocean to soothe her angst.

Cait came to a small fork in the road. If she continued to drive straight, she would wind along the cliffs and bypass Shane's house. If she took a right, she'd cut over the hills to Fiona's cottage. Cait stalled the car and turned her head between the two forks. With a soft curse, she drove her car straight, her heart hammering in her chest. Had she known that she would come here? To him?

Cait bit her lip as she drove closer to Shane's spread. Slowing her car to a crawl, she eyed his estate and debated turning into the drive. Shane's house was one of the most modern in the village, all sleek lines, dark wood and ceiling-height glass windows. Cait had never been inside though she was certain that the view had to be killer. The house perched proudly on a cliff, with windows wrapping three sides of the house to let the ocean breezes in. Behind, several stables and small outbuildings clustered around pastures lined with beautiful wood fences. To say that Shane was doing well for himself was an understatement.

Feeling foolish, Cait began to back her car away and slammed on her brakes when she heard the jaunty beep of a horn behind her. Glancing in her rearview mirror, she saw Shane's car pull up and then ease to a stop next to hers.

Caught, Cait gripped the wheel before turning to look at Shane through the open window.

"Stopping by?" Shane said and raised an eyebrow at her.

"Um, I was just out for a drive. So, you know, I can keep driving," Cait stammered.

"Okay," Shane said and smiled widely at her.

Damn it, Cait thought.

"I mean, unless, you, um, wanted company or something," Cait said lamely.

Shane chuckled. "Cait, can't you just say that you came to see me?"

"Can't you just make it easy on a woman?" Cait felt her temper rise and she almost threw her car into reverse.

"Yes, ma'am, come on in," Shane said and pulled his car up the paved drive.

Cait glared at his taillight and contemplated leaving. It wouldn't matter now. He knew that she had come to see him so that would give Shane the upper hand. Determined to regain her footing, she pulled her car behind his and parked. Shane leaned against his car with a small canvas bag in his hands. He crossed his arms and waited for her to get out of her car.

Crossing to him, Cait met his eyes stubbornly.

"Why aren't you at the pub?" Shane asked.

"I was in a bad mood and taking it out on the customers. I went for a drive to soothe my nerves and ended up here," Cait said.

"Well, well. I'm honored," Shane said. Picking her hand up, he brought it to his lips and traced a kiss over her palm. Cait felt her skin heat up. Shane's eyes narrowed into that look that men get when they focus on the object of their lust. Cait drew in a deep breath and shuddered it out.

Whoa, boy, she thought.

She wasn't sure when she had developed a crush on Shane. He'd always been the affable guy around town. He owned several properties, was a fair landlord, and went to church on Sundays. Nothing about him screamed sex, yet for some reason that was all Cait could think about when she was around him these days.

"Don't feel too special. You'll get over it once I say something to make you mad," Cait said breezily and pulled her hand from his to tuck it in her pocket. She nodded at the bag and raised an eyebrow.

"Ah, yes, for Baron. He's been acting odd for days. Doesn't want to run, won't eat much, I'm really worried about him," Shane said as concern creased his brow. Baron was his thoroughbred and Shane talked about him as if he was a son. Immediately concerned, Cait turned towards the stables.

"Let's go see him," Cait said. She was excited to explore the property as well.

"Sure," Shane said. As they crossed to the stables, they fell into an easy conversational rhythm as Cait peppered Shane with questions about the stables and how many animals he owned. Cait breathed in the scent of hay and horses and jumped as the lights automatically popped on when they walked into the gleaming building. Cait surveyed the clean stalls, dark wood, and open windows that peeked to the sea. The stable was stunning and Cait could tell that any animal housed here would be well cared for.

"Shane, your stable is gorgeous," Cait gushed as they walked down the main aisle towards a large stall at the end. A few shuffles and soft nickering came over the wall of the boxes and several horses poked their heads over their stalls to check out who had come into their home.

"Thank you, it's a passion of mine," Shane said softly.

Cait looked at him and warmth flooded through her. The heat in his eyes was unmistakable. If she was reading him right, then Shane had just as much passion for her as he did his horses.

"I can see that," Cait said and brushed her hand softly over the muzzle of a soft brown pony mare that had stuck her nose over the stall.

Reaching the last stall, they both peered over the edge to see Baron, a shining black thoroughbred, lying on the ground. Immediately concerned, Shane slid the stall door open. Baron struggled to get up but Shane pressed him down.

"Can you flip the extra lights on?" Shane asked and pointed to a small switch. Cait ran to it and light illuminated the stall. Gingerly, Cait stepped in and, disregarding her jeans, she kneeled at Baron's head.

"It's the weirdest thing. He won't go out in the pasture even when I leave his door open. Yet, I can't find anything visible on him. There is no indication of sickness. I've pressed my hands all over his body but can't seem to find any spots of pain. I'm at a loss," Shane said sadly.

Cait's heart raced. She knew that she had no choice but to use her power, but she wasn't ready to tell Shane about herself. Terrified that Shane would be scared of her, she stared blindly into the deep brown eyes of the proud horse. Her heart won out and she dropped her mental shields and reached out to Baron's mind.

"What's wrong, baby? Can you tell me what's hurting you?" Cait crooned to the horse and scratched behind his ears.

Shane laughed, "I wish that he could."

Cait ignored Shane and continued to stroke Baron's ears.

"My foot. Glass or something under the horseshoe. Infection. Hurt. Can't stand anymore," Baron thought. Cait almost jumped. Communicating with a horse was far different than with a dog. She wondered if their intelligence level was different. Thinking about how to tell Shane, she continued to stroke Baron.

"Why don't you go get him a carrot and see if he will perk up? I've learned a few things from Flynn's stable hands, maybe he'll let me check him out," Cait said.

"Don't do too much until I get back. He is still a very powerful horse, Cait," Shane cautioned and stepped from the box. Moving quickly, Cait bent to Baron's hooves.

"Which one?" she whispered and laid her hand on each of Baron's legs until Baron twitched.

"This one," Baron communicated.

Cait bent her head to look closely, confident that Baron wouldn't kick her. If she looked really close she could just see a little pus oozing from beneath the horseshoe affixed to Baron's hoof. It would be easy for anyone to miss.

"Cait! Get your head away from his hoof!" Shane instructed calmly, knowing not to shout and scare Baron.

"I found something, Shane," Cait said and sat back on her heels.

"You did?" Shane moved close and, keeping a watchful eye on Baron, he bent to kneel by Cait.

Cait pointed to where the pus oozed from his foot.

"See that? Something must be lodged beneath the shoe," Cait said.

"Well, damn, you are right, something is there. Shit, I wonder if I can get him to stand and walk to where I can pry the shoe off."

Cait stood and spoke directly to Baron.

"Baron, can you walk with us just out to the aisle? We are going to help you but we can't do it from in here," Cait asked.

Shane looked at her like she was crazy and then jumped as Baron shifted.

"Well, shit, he likes you," Shane laughed and helped Baron to his feet, leading him to the hookup in the stable.

Cait ducked under the lead ropes to nuzzle her head at Baron's. Shane moved quickly, not wanting to prolong the pain. In a matter of moments he had the shoe off and swore softly.

"Damn it, it looks like there is a piece of glass in here. Now how in the world would that have happened?"

Cait tapped into Baron's brain.

"Does any of the pasture run the length of the road? Kids throwing bottles from their cars?"

"It does actually and I haven't walked that way in a while. I need to get out there and check the fence line," Shane said, disgust with himself evident in his voice.

"Hey, don't worry, these things happen. Baron will be okay. Can you get the glass out?"

The horse shifted against Cait.

"Just did. Now I am going to put some antibiotic cream on it. It is fairly infected but Fiona makes a very powerful cream for me," Shane said.

Cait peered around Baron's head to look at Shane.

"You use Fiona's medicines?"

"Sure, why wouldn't I?"

"I don't know. Not sure if you believed in that," Cait said.

"Believed in what? Herbal remedies? Perfectly natural," Shane said and dusted his palms off. Standing, he came around to wrap his hands around Baron's head. "I'm sorry, buddy, extra carrots for you. You should be back to running the fields in no time."

The horse brushed his head against Shane's and Cait did a quick scan of Baron's mind to find him in a much better mood.

"I think he's feeling better already," Cait said.

Together, they led the horse back into the stable and crooned words of encouragement and love to the massive animal.

"I never knew that you were so good with horses," Shane commented as they left the stall. He placed a hand at the small of her back and Cait felt heat shoot through her entire body. Shane turned her the other direction and out of the stables, away from his house. As they left the stable, Cait gasped at the view.

"Oh, Shane, this is beautiful," Cait said. The world opened up below the stables, rolling away in pastures of lush green before diving into the blue waters of the ocean. Cait felt a little lightheaded as the rush of beauty swept through her.

"So are you," Shane said hoarsely and Cait gasped at the naked need in his eyes. Shane pulled her to his chest and slid his lips over her own. A shot of pure lust hit her stomach and she stumbled against Shane as she went dizzy from her need. Undeterred, Shane wrapped his arms

around her waist and pulled her up until Cait's legs strad-
dled him. Cait almost fainted at the aggressiveness of
Shane's move. She felt lightheaded and giddy and laughed
against Shane's mouth.

Taking it as an invitation for more, Shane dipped his
tongue between her lips. Cait felt herself moving and realized that Shane was walking her backwards. The scratch of
hay brushed against her legs and Cait guessed that Shane
had backed her into a pile of hay. She arched against him
as he slipped her butt onto a bale of hay so that he stood
between her legs. Shane groaned softly and broke the kiss,
trailing his lips down her neck to nibble at the sensitive
spot at her nape. Cait jerked against him and turned her
head to allow him to continue his explorations. A shiver
rushed through her as his lips brushed against her soft skin.
Craving more, she ran her hands up his strong arms to
thread her fingers through his thick hair. Swept under by
the emotions that ran through her, Cait could only hold on
as Shane took the lead.

In one smooth movement, Shane tugged on her tank
top and ripped it over her head. Cait trembled as she sat
before him half naked. She wanted him. Oh, did she want
him. A surge of need shot through Cait and her skin felt
like it was on fire. Her heart pounded in her chest and she
met Shane's lust-filled eyes. Cait had never had a man look
at her like this before. It filled her with confidence,
knowing that Shane wanted her as much as he did. For
once in her life, Cait felt powerful with a man, and she'd
never been more turned on. Shane's breath shuddered out
as he pierced her with his deep brown eyes, his hands
tracing her waist softly. Before she knew what was

happening, Shane bent and with one hand flicked the clasp of her bra open.

"Hey!" Cait gasped out.

Shane shot her a cocky grin and brought his mouth to her small breasts and liquid heat pooled deep in her core at the sensation of his mouth on her nipples. Cait moaned and let her head fall back against the hay as Shane pleasured her with his mouth. Wrapping her legs around his waist, she pulled him closer, craving contact. Shane groaned against her breasts and, bringing his head up, he captured her mouth with his and sucked hungrily at her lips. Cait ground her hips against him, suddenly desperate for release. She didn't want to think about what they were doing or where they were. She wanted Shane to make her world fall away, if even just for a moment.

"Hold on, Cait, just hold on," Shane whispered against her mouth and Cait whimpered into his lips as he unbuttoned her jeans and slipped a hand beneath her underwear to find her ready. Cait arched into his hand and in one smooth movement, Shane slipped his fingers inside of her. Shocked at the sensation, lust whiplashed through Cait and she shattered around his hand. Shane held her as she sobbed her release into his mouth, so happy, so alive for the first time in years.

Gently, Shane stroked her hair and held her close to him. Cait waited for his next move. Hearing him sigh, she pulled her head back to look at his face. Shane looked... almost stoic as he removed his hand from her pants and slipped her bra back up on her shoulders. Confused at the sudden change in him, Cait put her walls up.

She didn't know what was happening, but couldn't deal

with being on the blunt edge of rejection again. Quickly she fastened her bra and reached for her tank top, her mind whirling.

"Cait," Shane began.

"Just stop, I get it. You've got the blonde. So, we shouldn't be doing this. Fine, we are both adults, no big deal." Cait hopped off the bale of hay and pulled her tank top over her head, wanting to bury her face in its darkness for a moment. Standing straight, Cait patted Shane on the cheek, affecting a nonchalance that she certainly didn't feel.

"No, not that, not at all," Shane said.

"It's fine, I get it," Cait said and turned to walk away. She gasped as Shane whipped her back.

"No, you don't get it. I want more than the proverbial roll in the hay, as it were," Shane said, raising an eyebrow at her.

"Well, looks like that's all you'll get today, sailor. So why don't you just back off," Cait ordered. She had known it was stupid to come here. Looking around at all of the wealth that surrounded her, she heard her mother's words. *You're not good enough for all this. He only wants you as a side piece.*

"No, I won't back off. We have something here. I want more. I want you," Shane said directly, his eyes boring into her. Tears pricked her eyes and for just a moment, Cait allowed herself to imagine being with him. It would be wonderful. Thinking of the blonde, she knew that she wasn't in Shane's league.

"Sorry, Shane, but I just needed to blow off some steam. Thanks for being a friend," Cait said and kissed him lightly on the lips. This time when she turned, Shane didn't stop her.

"You're full of shite, Cait Gallagher. When you get it figured out, let me know," Shane said bitterly behind her. Cait didn't turn, just walked through the stables with tears blurring her vision. She heard Baron's soft whinny but kept walking, her back ramrod straight. She had a business to run.

CHAPTER 13

AIT GRASPED THE steering wheel blindly and without thinking, turned her car towards the cove. She shuddered as she thought about what she was driving away from. Trying to pull herself back from a crying jag, she steered her car down the lane from Fiona's house. She wasn't ready to face Fiona yet was too restless to go home. Inexplicably pulled towards the cove, Cait got out of her car and raced across the fields to stand at the top of the footpath that led to the cove.

Her breath shuddered out as she stared down at the waters that refused to reflect the sun's rays as it dipped towards the horizon. Finally answering the call of the cove, Cait followed the path that led down the side of the cliffs. She skidded to a halt at the sandy beach and remembered Fiona's instructions. Cait looked around desperately for some rocks or flowers…just something to give as a gift. Finding nothing, she pulled her wallet out of her purse and dug in the side pocket. Inside lay a small tarnished silver charm in the shape of a heart. It had been foolish of her to keep it all these years, Cait thought. The charm had fallen from a bracelet of her mother's and Cait had used to pretend that Sarah had given it to her as a gift.

Who was she kidding? Her mother never gave her gifts, Cait thought bitterly as she rolled the charm between her fingers. With a small sigh, she stepped onto the sand and slid her shoes off. Tracing a little circle, she stepped into it and felt the warm sand squish between her toes.

"Um, so, I'm here. I know that you want me to be. And I don't even know why I'm here. But, um, I offer you this gift and ask for protection while I am here. I mean the cove nor those who rest here any harm," Cait said. With a last look at the heart, she tossed it into the water, imagining its path to the bottom of the ocean mirroring that of her own sinking heart.

Cait waited quietly for something to happen. Silence greeted her. Slowly, the tension seemed to ease from her shoulders and Cait allowed herself to take in her surroundings. The sun was a warm ball of light that was sinking between the two rocky cliffs that hugged the cove, its light shooting to the canyon walls behind her. The water lapped gently at the sand and Cait took a few deep breaths before stepping closer to the edge of the water. When the water stayed the same, Cait smiled and allowed herself to enjoy the freedom of being on an empty beach.

Too keyed up to sit still, Cait began to walk the length of the beach. As Cait paced the soft sand of the beautiful beach, she tried not to cry. What had she been thinking? She had let her powerful attraction to Shane cloud her judgment.

"I want you. I want to be with you." Shane's words drifted through her mind. Had he meant that? What about the blonde? Cait wished that she had just asked him about his relationship with that woman.

It made Cait angry to think about Shane's hands on another woman when he'd just had them all over her body. She'd never been so viscerally attracted to a man before. Yet, Cait feared that her mother was right. Cait would never fit into Shane's world. She wasn't high society or anything fancy. The only thing she wanted was to run a good business, to travel, and to start a family someday.

The thought of a family made Cait skid to a stop. Did she want a family? She had never really given the idea that much thought. Perhaps because she didn't come from a traditional family unit, Cait rarely got those maternal urges that many of her friends seemed to get. Cait dipped her toes in the water and tried to imagine what her and Shane's baby would look like. She laughed softly at herself and shook her head. How could a pub owner even fit a baby into her schedule? Stupid, Cait thought.

"I gave birth on a ship in mid-battle. I'm quite certain you'll do just fine." A voice like molasses on a knife blade startled Cait. She whipped around and her heart simply stopped. Just for a beat. When Cait could drag a breath in again, she turned her head to look for help.

"I mean you no harm, little one. You're of my blood, after all," the voice said.

The ghost? Vision? Apparition? Stood across from Cait on the sand. She seemed almost human but there was a soft translucence to the skin that showed that she wasn't of this world. In the time between day and night, the veil between worlds grew thin. Grace O'Malley stood before her, a proud woman with beautiful eyes, in an ancient dress.

"Grace?" Cait whispered.

"Of course! Who else would walk my cove?" Grace tossed her hair arrogantly and eyed the cove as though she owned it. Which she did, Cait thought.

"You're stunning," Cait said, unable to help herself.

"Why, thank you, little one. It is nice to know that my beauty holds. But, I must go before the sun slips into the sea. Why did you come here tonight?"

"I...I don't really know. It was like I was drawn here," Cait admitted.

"Ah, and your feelings? They are full of sorrow...and, I'm not sure the word today...inferiority perhaps?" Grace tilted her head and eyed Cait.

Cait flushed at the assessment and nodded.

"Um, yes, I suppose inferiority would be close. Insecurity is really the word we use now," Cait said.

"And you feel inferior to a man?" Grace raised an eyebrow incredulously.

"Well, not really. Yes and no. I feel like I can never really step into his world, he is so rich and I am barely getting by," Cait admitted. She shrugged her shoulders helplessly.

"Is that so? And that is the only thing that is holding you back from this man?" Grace put her hands on her hips and waited.

Cait gulped and raised her hands before letting them drop to her sides. She felt like she was at a therapist's office or something of the like.

"I, okay, no, it probably isn't just the money," Cait said. Grace waited silently.

"Okay, fine. I just don't see myself in relationships. I was raised in a bad household, I didn't have an example of a good relationship growing up, and I just don't really know how to do it. If…if I can do it at all," Cait whispered. Tears pricked her eyes. Surprised, she dashed them away quickly with her knuckles.

"Ah, yes. There we have it," Grace said.

"Yes, there you have it," Cait said forlornly.

"Do you think that you are not worthy of love?" Grace asked.

"What? No, I mean, of course I am." Cait's head shot up and she met Grace's eyes.

"Do you not think that you are a bright and interesting person?"

"Well, sure I am," Cait said.

"One that is capable of running a business, interacting and dare I say…having relationships with hundreds of customers on a regular basis?"

"Yes." Cait nodded.

"One that has lifelong friendships?"

"Yes, ma'am," Cait said.

"And a woman that is descended from my own blood…a blood that ran in the bones of one of the proudest women in the history of Ireland? I chose my suitors. Never did I wait for them to choose me nor did I wonder if I was good enough. I knew that I was deserving of love and picked based on that alone. You, my dear, are of my blood and are powerful beyond belief. Choose, my little one, choose love," Grace said before fading silently into the darkness as the sun slipped below the edge of the water.

Cait's mouth hung open and she gaped at where Grace had stood. Whirling around, she faced the water to see a faint blue glow emanating from the depths of the cove. A shiver ran through her. But, instead of fear, it was power. Cait smiled and nodded at the water. She knew an ass-kicking when she saw one.

"Okay, Grace, duly noted. I'll do my best to make you proud," Cait said to the water and laughed as the light brightened for a moment. Cait raced to the path before she lost all light for the climb back to the top of the cliffs.

Cait was overwhelmed with the enormity of what had just happened. Was this why the cove had called to her for so long? Had Grace always wanted to meet up with her? Cait wondered if Grace was just a figment of her imagination. Maybe the stress of the day had caught up with her and tipped her over into crazytown, she thought with a soft laugh.

She'd always been one to dismiss her gift, as well as all of the mysticism that surrounded Grace's Cove. And yet... tonight had been undeniable proof of what was. Quite simply, Cait couldn't argue her away around what had just happened. A strange sense of joy filled her. It was almost as if having the ghost of Grace O'Malley claim Cait as her own gave her a sense of belonging that her mother had never been able to impart to her. Mulling over Grace's words, Cait made her way across the fields to her car. She saw the light glowing in Fiona's cottage. Knowing that Fiona would see her emotions, but unable to stop herself,

Cait drove the short distance to check in on the old woman.

"Why, Cait! So good to see you!" Fiona said as she opened the heavy wooden door. Pulling the door open wider, she gestured for Cait to step into the cottage. Cait bent to give the old woman a brief hug and worried that her bones seemed frail.

"What brings you here?" Fiona stepped back and assessed Cait carefully. Her face fell as she got a read on Cait's emotions. "Oh, poor girl. Your mother?"

For what seemed like the gazillionth time that day, tears jumped into Cait's eyes. Cait nodded once before allowing Fiona to wrap her arms around her.

"I don't know why I let her get to me," Cait whispered into Fiona's neck.

"Because she is your mother and she'll always get to you," Fiona said briskly and stepped back, patting her shoulder. She motioned to her two wooden rocking chairs tucked in an alcove of the cozy room. "Come, sit. Whiskey?"

Cait nodded and made her way to a rocking chair, slipping into the worn wood seat and allowing the arms to envelop her. She stared blindly into the flickering flames of the small fire that Fiona had going in the stove. Though it was warm out, the fire provided just enough heat to keep the cottage cozy, not unbearable.

Fiona handed Cait a small glass of whiskey and settled into the seat next to her. They held their glasses in the air.

"Slàinte," Cait said and admired the way the whiskey caught the light of the fire before taking a healthy sip. The liquid burned a trail to her stomach and she allowed the familiar comfort to ease the tension in her shoulders. Never a big drinker, she'd always enjoyed a single glass of whiskey at the end of the night to wind down.

"I saw Grace," Cait blurted out as Fiona began to speak.

"What? When?" Fiona said, deterred from asking about Cait's mother.

"Um, just now. At the cove," Cait said and fidgeted with her jeans. Her mind was still reeling from what she had seen though Cait swore that her heart felt stronger because of the encounter.

"Why, that is just wonderful. She rarely appears anymore, you know," Fiona said and looked carefully at Cait. "You must have been in a fair level of distress then for her to appear."

"I suppose that I was," Cait demurred.

"Your mother? Or something else?"

"I…I don't know. All of it, I guess. My mother. Shane. Life. My ability or lack thereof to handle normal relation-ships," Cait said and shrugged her shoulders.

"Ah, I see. That's quite a lot for one evening," Fiona said.

Cait huffed out a laugh. "Yes, yes it's been quite a day indeed."

"And what did Grace have to say about it all?"

"She pretty much gave me a kick in the ass along the lines of… 'no descendent of mine is unworthy of anything…don't you know how awesome I am?'" Cait laughed into her whiskey. There was no denying that Grace O'Malley was one tough cookie.

"Yes, that certainly sounds like her. No time for

sniveling or bemoaning your fate on her watch," Fiona laughed at Cait.

"Why does the cove glow blue?" Cait blurted out.

"Oh! Well, now, isn't that interesting?" Fiona smiled widely at Cait. Cait felt a little like a mouse about to be pounced on by a hungry cat.

"Is it? I thought that I was imagining things the other night but then I saw it again today," Cait said.

"What night? When did you see it?" Fiona swatted away today's occurrence.

"Um, well, at Keelin's wedding. I walked down there to catch some air," Cait said.

"And with whom did you walk?"

"I was alone," Cait said staunchly.

"Liar," Fiona said smoothly and Cait laughed.

"Ah, lord save me from women with mystical powers!" Cait said.

"Oh, it wasn't my powers, my dear. The cove only glows blue in the presence of love. Today would make sense as Grace loves you…but the wedding?" Fiona raised her eyebrow and took a small sip of her whiskey.

Cait felt heat creep up her cheeks at the mention of love. So, that was the secret to the glow, she mused. Part of her felt a sense of awe at being loved by a ghost and the other part of her felt sick to her stomach as she thought about being in love with Shane.

"Shane came to find me. He was worried about me being too close to the edge and having been drinking," Cait whispered.

She jumped as Fiona clapped her hands and laughed.

"Perfect! Love it is. Now, go get your man and tell him

what you are," Fiona said. Cait stared at her as if she had grown two heads.

"I…what? I can't go get him and I certainly can't tell him about…this," Cait said and pointed to her head.

"Why not?" Fiona asked.

"Because…because…it's insanity, is what it is," Cait stuttered out.

"The Donovans don't seem to think so," Fiona said, referencing the couple that Cait had helped.

"Yeah, but I don't have to live with them. Imagine any man wanting to be with me once he knows that I can read his every thought if I want," Cait said furiously. Her old feelings of not being good enough bubbled to the surface.

"You won't know that until you ask," Fiona said.

"Yeah, I can pretty much guarantee you that's a no," Cait said and stood to go.

"I don't think that you give Shane enough credit," Fiona said and Cait stopped.

"It's not that I don't give him credit. It's just that…no man could put up with this," Cait said helplessly.

"No normal man. But this man loves you. Don't you think that is enough?"

"I don't know if I believe in love," Cait said stubbornly.

"Ah, well, then. I suppose you know it all," Fiona said serenely and pulled out her knitting basket.

"I didn't say that. I just…listen, it's been a long day and I just wanted to check on you," Cait said, standing over Fiona's chair.

"No need to check on me, dear. I'm not the one having a breakdown," Fiona said. She accepted Cait's kiss on her papery cheek without comment and Cait made a beeline for the door.

Having a breakdown? Cait scoffed at the idea and turned the music all the way up to drown out her thoughts on the way back into the village.

CHAPTER 14

CAIT WOKE EARLY after another fitful night of sleep. Seeing as though she was feeling broody, she knew nothing could be better than some girl talk to kick her out of it. Since Keelin was out of town, Aislinn would be the next logical choice. Checking the time, Cait saw that she had at least an hour before Aislinn's shop opened.

Cait eyed her apartment. She lived a fairly minimalist lifestyle, so there wasn't much in the way of cleaning to occupy her. Picking up a stack of papers, she ran through her list of bills and inventory for the pub. Finding everything up to date, she sighed and eyed the kitchen. She rarely baked, except if she was in a mood. If she baked now, then she would be acknowledging that Shane had put her in a mood, Cait thought stubbornly. Then she thought about Aislinn's lovely homemade tea and knew that her scones would go perfectly with it. Sighing, she rose and walked to her pantry.

An hour later, Cait wiped her brow and stared down at

her perfect cinnamon raisin scones. The scent made her mouth water and she was tempted to take a bite now. Instead, she tucked them in a small cloth-lined basket and went to change her clothes. Realizing that her mind was more at ease now, she smiled as she brushed a hint of the wedding makeup on and fluffed her short curls. Cait picked out a bright red tank to lighten her mood and threw on Aislinn's pretty beaded necklace. Checking her watch, she grabbed her basket and left her apartment, her mind already on things to do for the day.

The morning sunshine greeted her and Cait waved hello to a few people on the street. The crisp sea air stole up the road from the water and Cait drew in a big breath. She never tired of this view. She loved her small village fiercely and was determined to hold her own with her pub there for many years to come. Whistling a bit, she strolled down the hill, passing colorful shops and markets along the way. She smiled at the tourists lined up and waiting for their tickets to the harbor cruises. Tourism was good for their village, as were the free drink tickets she gave out to the passengers of the boat cruise. Reaching Aislinn's shop, Cait stopped to admire her most recent window display.

Instead of her usual lace doilies and charming water-colors, Aislinn had lined the window with edgy black-and-white photos of everyday Irish life. Cait had to hand it to her, Aislinn certainly had an eye for catching the heart of Ireland. Seeing a picture of Gallagher's pub with an old man leaning against the building with a pipe, Cait sighed. Of course she would have to buy that for the pub now. A soft tinkle of bells rang out as Cait pushed the door open.

Cait stopped mid-stride as she took in the scene before

her. Aislinn was giggling and tucking her hair behind her ear while talking to a man that Cait had never seen before. Cait's mouth dropped open as cool and calm Aislinn all but preened for the gentleman she was speaking to. Aislinn didn't even glance towards the door, so Cait took her time and circled quietly, trying to get a look at the man discreetly. She moved to a stack of hand-painted postcards and peered around it to take in the new visitor that was making Aislinn all aflutter.

Tall, dark, and yum, was all Cait could think as she scanned the neatly dressed man. Brown hair cut close to his scalp accented light gray eyes tucked behind trim wire-framed glasses. Cait gave a soft sigh. There was just something about glasses on a good-looking man. Checking out the rest of the package, Cait determined that though he appeared fairly preppy and orderly, his body filled out his well-cut suit. She would place money that he had at least a six-pack under that prim button down shirt. With no qualms at all, Cait let down her shields and reached out to his mind.

A psychiatrist? Hmm, now wasn't that interesting, Cait thought. She watched as he spoke quietly to Aislinn about a black-and-white photo. Cait didn't have to read his mind to see his interest in Aislinn. Hoping that this could finally be the one for Aislinn, Cait made her way across the shop.

"Hello, there. You must be new in town," Cait said and held out her free hand to the man, who jumped slightly at her words.

"Ah, yes, that I am," the man said as he held out his hand automatically.

"Cait Gallagher, cousin to this beautiful lady," Cait said cheerfully.

"Baird Delaney," Baird said and turned to smile at Aislinn, frank male appreciation in his eyes.

Cait gulped as her mouth went dry. Whoa, boy, if she wasn't already hooked on Shane she would go for the delicious doctor herself.

"I'm Aislinn, nice to meet you," Aislinn said automatically.

"Well, yes, we met a few moments ago," Baird said teasingly and Aislinn blushed.

Cait's mouth dropped open. She couldn't remember ever having seen Aislinn blush before.

"Right, of course," Aislinn stammered.

Cait took pity on her.

"So, Baird, are you visiting from…?"

"I'm in from Galway, but actually, I plan to set up my psychiatry practice here for a while. I just rented the office building down by the water with the apartment above it." Baird gestured towards the water.

"Ah, yes, a right fine building. Good landlord, as well," Cait said. That building was owned by Shane and Cait had always admired it.

"Yes, he's great. We are going to grab a beer at Gallagher's Pub this weekend." Baird smiled.

"Well, then, I certainly hope you enjoy the experience. Best pub in town," Cait said and smiled widely at Baird.

Aislinn elbowed her.

"It's her pub, so of course she'd say that," Aislinn said.

"Is it? How interesting. I had assumed that a man

owned it. Now it is even more appealing," Baird said with an easy smile for Cait.

"That's right. I run a fine establishment. As does Aislinn. Isn't her work lovely?" Cait wanted to shift the conversation back to Aislinn as she could tell that Aislinn was getting jealous.

"It is. I was hoping to purchase a few of these prints for my new office," Baird said as he gestured to several of the prints that he had picked from the walls.

"Right fine choices you've made there," Cait said as she admired the pictures.

The conversation stalled for a moment. Cait cleared her throat.

"Um, I'll just be putting these scones back in the court-yard. Would you like to join us for tea, Dr. Delaney?" Cait said.

"Baird, please. Some other time; I need to get unpacked," Baird said.

"Ah, well then, I'll be seeing you this weekend for a pint then," Cait said with an easy smile and swung the basket jauntily from her elbow as she moved into Aislinn's small courtyard that was tucked behind her shop. Cait found herself humming as she set up plates on the long picnic table in the middle of the yard. Well, wasn't this interesting? It would be fun to watch Aislinn in a romance. She'd yet to see her cousin truly open her heart to anyone.

At home in Aislinn's space, Cait stepped into the kitchen to set water to heat before taking cups and napkins back to the table. Sitting down, Cait stretched her legs out and leaned back to let the sun warm her skin, knowing that Aislinn would bring the water and tea to meet her shortly.

"I'm dying." Aislinn's voice broke through Cait's relaxation. Cait smiled up at her cousin as she hurried to Cait with a teapot.

"Dying to jump him? Yummmm," Cait said with a laugh.

"I can't even...I've never been so flustered before," Aislinn said with real concern on her face. Cait sat up and studied her face.

"I thought that you liked him?" Cait said.

"I...I do. I've just never felt such a powerful attraction so quickly," Aislinn said as she poured tea into the cups.

"But, isn't that a good thing?"

"Not with a psychiatrist! Could you imagine? Me... constantly scatterbrained and lost in my art and him all precise and wanting to analyze things?" Aislinn visibly shuddered. "It would be hell."

"Come on now, you don't know that. He seemed nice," Cait said and scooped some fresh cream onto her plate before uncovering her scones and placing them on the plates.

Aislinn grabbed her scone and bit into it distractedly.

"I don't know, Cait. It was like...I couldn't even read him, I was so blinded by his aura. There was no objectivity at all." Aislinn gestured with her scone.

"Hmm, sounds hot," Cait said jokingly.

"It's not. It's scary. I don't know how to handle that type of feeling," Aislinn admitted worriedly.

"Have you ever been in love before?" Cait asked.

"No, not really. Passionate relationships? Yes. But never love, not really." Aislinn shrugged her shoulders and stared across the courtyard.

"I think that I might be," Cait whispered.

Aislinn perked up immediately.

"Shane? Yes!"

"Well, yes, who else?" Cait said.

"So, did you sleep with him yet?"

"What? No, not yet, at least. I think that he is dating someone else," Cait admitted and filled Aislinn in on what had happened yesterday. Aislinn fanned her face mockingly.

"Wow, that's some hot stuff, Cait. It doesn't sound like the blonde is in the picture; why don't you just read his mind?" Aislinn said.

"Well, that's my other problem. Fiona wants me to tell him about me," Cait said.

"Oh," Aislinn said quietly.

"See! I knew that you would get it. Fiona thinks it is no big deal and that he'll love me anyway. I think it's a really big deal," Cait said as she brandished her scone in front of her face.

"Well, sure. He might not want you knowing his every thought," Aislinn said.

"Exactly."

"Can you tell him that you put blocks up so you don't hear everything?" Aislinn knew how Fiona had trained Cait to survive with her ability years ago.

"Ha…right. He'll already be halfway out the door by then," Cait said bitterly.

"I don't know. I don't think so. Shane is pretty level-headed. I think that he would hear you out," Aislinn said.

"I don't know what to do. I'm not used to being this torn up."

Aislinn reached out and squeezed her arm.

"I know, I can see it all over you. And, you didn't even tell me about your mom but I can read it a mile away. Bad?"

"Bad. We are done," Cait said softly.

"Well, good riddance to that crazy old bat," Aislinn said firmly, startling a laugh from Cait.

"Thanks, Aislinn. This is exactly what I needed. Now, promise you'll come to see me this weekend when Dr. Yum comes to visit," Cait said.

"Maybe. I don't know," Aislinn demurred. The tinkling of her front-door bells stopped her from saying more and she stood to go greet her new customer.

"Saved by the bell!" Cait yelled after her and stood to clear the table.

CHAPTER 15

S HANE FOUND HIMSELF staring out of the window
    for what seemed like the millionth time that day.
With a sigh, he pushed his papers aside and propped his
face in his hands. It had been three days since Cait had
turned her back on him at his farm. He felt like he'd been
kicked in the gut and had barely been able to eat this week.

Like some lovesick puppy, he scoffed to himself.

He'd been forward with her, Shane thought. He'd done
the things that a man was supposed to do when he wanted
a real relationship with a woman. Shane had bought her
flowers and deliberately didn't let things get out of hand at
his stables. A small tug of lust hit him as he thought about
Cait's trim body under his hands. Jesus, she was a fire-
cracker, Shane thought.

Shane rose and went to stand at the window of his
office. The water was a dazzling azure today and he longed
to be out with the fishermen, away from the headaches of
his work. Shane sighed and ran a hand through his hair.

What was with this week? It was like everything was

falling down around him. He'd had Cait very literally in the palm of his hand and seconds later she was gone. And, now, his real-estate properties in Galway were mysteriously operating at a loss. He'd gone over the figures until his eyes blurred. Yet he'd been unable to find any discrepancy in the numbers.

Staring at the water, Shane imagined taking Cait out in the boat he planned to buy. He could all but see her at the helm, wind tousling her curls, urging him to go faster. He'd never met a woman like her before, all moods, laughter, and heart. Life before Cait seemed to dull in comparison. Shane sighed and shrugged his shoulders. This wouldn't be his first setback with Cait. Maybe he just needed to push harder.

Checking his watch, he realized that he was going to be late for the meeting with his manager to discuss the real-estate properties in Galway. Shane chuckled softly. If Cait had only given him the chance to explain about the blonde he could have told her that she was his employee, not his date. Though, Shane had kind of enjoyed her reaction.

The laugh died on Shane's lips. Though he enjoyed knowing that Cait was jealous, he also hated knowing that she was hurting. He'd tossed and turned almost the entire night after she had left. His body burned for her. His pride was another matter. Just how many times would he let Cait push him away before he gave up, Shane wondered.

Shoving the papers from his desk into a folder, Shane hit the lights and went to meet Ellen, his manager, for dinner.

CHAPTER 16

C AIT CHECKED HER watch and got up for the second time to leave her apartment. Again, she hesitated. For years, she had stopped at Flynn's restaurant to pick up a Friday-night dinner for her mother. This week was different. Would Sarah expect her to bring dinner again? Or had she meant what she had said? Torn, Cait paced her living room.

Loyalty won out and with a sigh, Cait slipped a scarf over her shoulders. Friday night at the pub promised to be busy, and feeling a little down, Cait had decided to dress up a bit. In lieu of her typical jeans and tank top, she'd pulled on a fitted black skirt that ended far above her knees and a deep turquoise top. With a small smile, she'd pulled long, sparkly earrings from her jewelry box and put them on, admiring how they lined her face and swung below the line of her hair. With a last glance in the mirror to make sure that she'd applied her makeup the way that she'd been instructed, Cait left her apartment.

The sun hung low on the horizon, coating the village in

a warm glow. Cait smiled at the various couples walking the street, looking for a pint and bite to eat. Trying not to think of the potential confrontation in front of her, Cait focused on the beauty of Grace's Cove on her walk.

Reaching Flynn's restaurant, Cait just shook her head. *That man has a knack for business,* was all she could think. A line twenty deep wound from the front door and several couples sat at outside picnic benches, enjoying a glass of wine in front of the harbor before dinner. She breezed past the front door and walked around the back to the kitchen door.

Sultry scents of garlic and butter reached her nose and Cait all but moaned. Flynn's restaurants were known across the country for the freshest seafood around. Cait knew that much of it came from the un-fished Grace's Cove. Most of Ireland was convinced that the cove was cursed and few dared to enter there, which made Flynn's daily catch even more precious.

"Aye, hullo there, Cait!" Terry, the chef, shouted to her from his stance at the grill.

"Hiya, Terry, how's Sharon?"

"Glowing, due any day! I'll be sure to bring the little one past the pub when he arrives," Terry said cheerfully. His first son was due to arrive any day.

"I look forward to that. I'll get him his first pint." Cait winked at him.

"To help him sleep, of course! I've got your order here." Terry nodded towards the bag of food on the counter.

"Thanks, Terry. Put it on my tab," Cait said and snagged the bag, easing carefully from the kitchen so as not to disturb the busy dance of the servers that rushed in and out.

Cait hefted the bag and walked past the window of the restaurant that was open to the sea breeze. She froze in her tracks. Shane sat at a cozy table for two, pouring a glass of wine for the blonde. He looked happy and relaxed, Cait thought. Envy filled her as the blonde laughed at something that he said and Shane gestured wildly with his hands to make a point.

Feeling sick to her stomach, Cait watched for a moment, frozen with anger and sadness. Just as she was about to turn away, Shane saw her.

"Cait!" Shane said from inside the restaurant.

Cait could only stare at him and shake her head. "No."

"Cait, wait!" Shane got up from the table.

Feeling foolish, Cait turned and ran around the back of the restaurant, berating herself for even bothering to stop for food for her mother. This whole week had just been stupid, she thought stubbornly. Picking up the pace, she made her way towards the street, hoping that Shane wouldn't follow.

"Seriously, Cait? You're running from me?" Shane panted behind her and latched onto her arm.

Cait's heart pounded in her chest. She took a deep breath, trying to calm herself. No need to get angry, she had nothing permanent with Shane, Cait thought. Pasting a smile on her face, she turned to him.

"I'm sorry, I need to get into work, Shane. No time for chatting," Cait said brightly.

"You're picking up food for Sarah?" Shane said, his eyebrows raised in disbelief.

Cait stomped her foot and raised her chin a bit. "So? What's it to you?"

"Oh, I don't know, maybe the fact that she ripped out your heart earlier this week would make me wonder why you would bring her food."

"She's my mother," Cait said, shrugging her shoulders helplessly.

"She's not a mother," Shane said fiercely.

"It's really none of your business, Shane," Cait said furiously. She felt like a fool getting caught bringing food to Sarah after the way that Sarah had treated her.

"None of my business, is it? When you cry all over me about her?"

"Hey, I didn't come running to you! You came to me," Cait all but shouted at him. Craning her eyes around at the sidewalks, she lowered her voice.

"Perhaps that was my mistake," Shane said stiffly.

"Well, either way, she's all I've got. I can't leave her," Cait said.

"She's not all you've got, you've got me," Shane said softly, his heart in his eyes. Cait squeezed her eyes shut against the unexpected clench in her heart.

"I don't at that, do I?" Cait nodded her head towards the restaurant where the blonde waited for him.

"Cait, Ellen's my employee, not my date," Shane said tersely.

Cait gaped at the restaurant for a moment as the real- ization that Shane hadn't been two-timing her settled over her. Warmth flooded her cheeks, and though she felt embarrassed, she couldn't help but smile stupidly at Shane.

"Really?"

"Yes, really. I just took her to the wedding because I needed a date," Shane said.

Cait dug her toe into the ground and tried not to do a happy dance. She hadn't realized just how much it had hurt her to see Shane with another woman. Feeling awkward, she looked down at her feet.

"So, now what?' Cait said.

"Now you apologize and tell me that you can't wait to go on a date with me."

"What! Apologize for what?" Cait demanded, meeting Shane's eyes.

"Um, how about apologizing for walking out on me at my stables...and in the condition that I was in?" Shane said, deliberately referencing their sexy moment.

Cait felt a warm hum start to throb through her as she thought about that day and his hands all over her body. Unconsciously, she licked her lips.

"Oh, I see that you're trying to tease me now," Shane said, his eyes fastened on her lips. Cait hiccupped out a giggle.

"I, no, I'm not. I swear. But, I certainly don't owe you an apology as I was operating under the assumption that you were with the blonde," Cait said, still refusing to say Ellen's name.

Shane stepped close, until their bodies almost touched. Forced to look up into his eyes, Cait gulped.

"You know what they say about assumptions," Shane said softly, his lips hovering dangerously close to hers.

"That they make an ass out of you?" Cait said deliberately, poking him.

"You and me, Cait, You and me," Shane said and

eased his lips over hers softly. Cait sighed into his mouth and swayed against him, allowing herself to feel the warmth of this moment. His lips teased hers softly and when Cait moaned into his mouth, Shane slipped his tongue between her lips to tease her. Heat shot through Cait.

A wolf whistle from across the street interrupted the moment and Cait jumped, realizing where she was. Stepping back from Shane she gathered herself, refusing to turn and see who had whistled.

Shane pinned Cait with his eyes.

"I'll stop by the pub later. We can pick this up after?" Shane asked.

"I'm not that kind of girl, Shane, you'll need to wine and dine me just like your fancy Galway ladies," Cait said cheekily and turned away, feeling a lightness enter her that hadn't been there all week.

"I'll be sure to do that, Cait Gallagher. Save a dance for me later," Shane said.

Grateful that she'd decided to dress up this evening, Cait put an extra bump into her hips as she walked away, knowing the view would be nice. Hearing his soft curse, she chuckled to herself. Oh, this was going to be fun.

Cait hummed to herself up the hill and towards her mother's apartment. The light feeling stayed with her all the way until she was about to buzz her mother's door. Nervous now, she fumbled a bit with her bags before finally buzzing the door.

"Who is it?"

"Ma, it's me, with your fish," Cait said nervously.

Silence answered her. Cait was about to turn away

when the door buzzed. With her stomach in knots, Cait climbed the stairs.

Sarah stood at the door, looking disheveled. Cait wondered when the last time she had left her apartment had been. She held up the bag of food silently to her mother.

"Yes, bring it in, put it on the table." Sarah gestured to the table in the middle of the room. Cait walked in and put the bag down. She turned towards her mother and waited silently for the typical invitation for her to sit.

Sarah averted her gaze and stood by the open door.

"So, it's like that, then? You'll take my food but won't invite me to sit?" Cait said bitterly. Not caring anymore, she let her shields down and reached out to her mother's mind. Finding a mass of confusion and anger, Cait jumped. Her mother didn't know what she felt and was certainly slipping towards crazy. When had Sarah's mind started to decline? Feeling a little less angry, Cait walked to her and patted her arm.

"Okay, Mom. I'll let you be. Enjoy your dinner," Cait said.

"Is this the devil's food?" Sarah said, gesturing towards the bag.

"No, Mom. You can feel that for yourself, can't you?" Cait asked.

Sarah reached out and clutched Cait's arm.

"I can feel that you've been with him. The rich one. You'll never make him happy. He'll plant his seed in you and leave you forever, especially when he finds out you're touched by the devil. You'll be stuck with a bastard child, just as I was," Sarah hissed, staring over Cait's shoulder.

Cait felt a shiver run through her. Her happiness dashed, she allowed the insecurity to creep back in. Maybe her mom was right, she thought. Shane might not want anything to do with her bloodline. He could easily leave her.

Feeling hopeless, Cait gently removed her mother's hand from her arm.

"Enjoy your dinner, I have to get to work," Cait said quietly and left without a backward glance.

She stepped into the crisp night air and drew a shaky breath. Nothing like being called the devil's spawn to get a Friday night started, Cait thought ruefully. She knew that she was good and not evil. Cait also knew that the time approached where she would have to figure out a place for her mother to stay. Sarah was moving towards needing some sort of daily assistance. Thinking of the cost of care for her mother, Cait shuddered and picked up her pace to the pub. It may be a few more years than Cait had thought before she could purchase the pub's building.

CHAPTER 17

*C*AIT GRABBED ANOTHER pint glass from the shelf as she kept her eye on the Guinness that she was currently building. Pulling the full glass from under the tap, she put it aside to settle and replaced it with the empty. Hand on the glass, she lifted her eyes to scan the length of the bar.

Patrons clustered around the bar, waiting their turn. The smaller pub tables scattered around the bar were full. Across the room, the band set up and the dinner tables had been pushed against the walls to make room for dancing. They had a good band tonight and people were already pouring in the door to get a spot.

Cait smiled at Patrick as he breezed past her, hands full of Harp bottles. He'd really turned into a valuable employee. Cait was glad that they had moved past their little misunderstanding. Seeing Aislinn enter the pub, Cait motioned her towards the far end of the bar.

"That'll be eight euros," Cait said and slid the Guinness glasses across the bar. Making change, she sidled down the bar and moved her stuff away from the seat she had saved for Aislinn.

"Bulmers?" Cait asked as Aislinn settled on the chair.

"Yes, thank you." Aislinn smiled up at her. Cait noticed that Aislinn had taken time with her appearance tonight. Her curvy body was tucked into a pretty red dress and a deep purple necklace popped against her throat.

"You look nice," Cait called to Aislinn, her eyebrows raised.

"As do you," Aislinn said, gesturing to Cait's outfit. Cait just shrugged and both women laughed at each other. They both knew exactly what they were about, Cait thought.

Cait slid Aislinn's glass across the bar. "Catch up with you in a bit," Cait said as she nodded to the cluster of people around the bar.

Cait fell into the rhythm of her pub and the tension in her shoulders eased. She ran a good establishment and was proud of her work here. She tapped her foot as a tin whistle picked up a lively beat and the crowd began to clap. Cait kept her eye on the bar as she filled glasses, wiped down tables, and made conversation with the locals. When the door opened and Shane stepped in, Cait could have sworn that the temperature in the room went up a notch.

Shane had changed after dinner and now wore a fitted button-down plaid shirt with the sleeves rolled up to reveal tanned arms. Dark jeans fit his legs nicely and Cait couldn't help but take a glance at his bum as he turned to hug an old woman by the front of the door. Behind him, Baird blinked into the melee, looking somewhat taken aback. Today he wore a fitted black t-shirt that revealed what Cait had suspected – an exceptionally muscular chest. Cait sliced a glance at Aislinn and grinned at her cousin's slightly dazed expression.

As if on cue, the two men turned and zeroed in on them. Cait's heart skipped a beat as Shane crossed the room to her. Without hesitation, he snagged her hand off of the bar and pressed a kiss to her palm. Cait felt heat creep up her cheeks and snatched her hand back. She propped her hands on her hips and tilted her head at Shane.

"You think that you can just walk in here and skip these fine gentleman?" Cait said and gestured to three old-timers that sat on the stools in front of her.

"Skip them? Why, of course not. I was coming to offer them a pint," Shane said and the men all cheered Shane affably. Cait couldn't conceal her grin as she stepped to build more pints of Guinness for the men.

Cait watched as Baird moved to Aislinn and smiled down at her. Aislinn's hands fluttered in front of her face and Cait finished building the pints, laughing softly to herself. She'd never seen Aislinn so distressed over a man before. This was going to be fun to watch.

Cait worked her way through the bar, filling pints, pouring shots, and mixing drinks. After an hour, she cut a glance to Patrick.

"I'm taking a break, you got this?"

"Yes, ma'am. Show them how it's done, Cait," Patrick said as he nodded towards the dance floor. Cait just rolled her eyes at him and poured herself a half-pint of Bulmers. Aislinn had snagged a table near the dance floor for her and the men. Cait moved through the crowd, smiling and cracking jokes with the regulars until she got to the table. With a sigh, she plopped down into the chair that Shane had pulled out for her.

"Slàinte," Cait said and raised her glass to the table. Cait noticed that Baird kept glancing in Aislinn's direction and that her cousin was uncharacteristically quiet.

"So, Baird, how have things been for you this week?" Cait shouted over the music.

"Oh, you've met Baird?" Shane said, eyebrow raised.

"I have at that," Cait said with a cocky tilt to her head.

"We met at Aislinn's shop," Baird offered quickly.

"He rented my second-favorite building from you," Cait said and saw Shane's shoulders ease.

Relaxing back into his chair, Shane eyed her. "I only rent to great tenants."

"Well, I don't plan to be a tenant forever," Cait mumbled. Shane sat up and leaned close to her.

"Is that so? What do you plan to do? Buy the building?" Shane scoffed at her.

Cait felt her temper whiplash through her and she raised her chin at him. Meeting his eyes, she took a slow sip of Bulmers before answering.

"Aye, I do."

"Ha, that will take you forever," Shane said dismissively.

A frisson of anger washed through Cait.

"Oh, I'm sorry, master. Us paupers can't have dreams?" Cait said angrily.

She shoved back from the table and ignoring Shane, stepped onto the dance floor where she was immediately swept into the rhythm of step dancing. The steps as natural as breathing, Cait flowed into the repetition of hops and kicks that categorized traditional Irish step dancing. She laughed as the line of dancers moved forward and back, meeting up with partners, and circling away. Cait raised her chin as her next turn brought her face to face with Shane.

As seasoned of a dancer as she, Shane kept pace with her as their feet pounded the floor in time to the pipes and banjo that played voraciously around them. Cait stared Shane down as they both moved hypnotically to the beat, heat rising between them as they danced in step. Not even realizing that the dance floor had formed a circle around them, Cait stayed with Shane and matched him turn for turn, bounce for bounce. Together, they bounded through the song until they were both panting, in lust, and very aware. On an oath, Shane grabbed Cait to him and captured her lips with his own.

Shocked, her heart hammering in her chest, Cait tried to pull away. Shane increased the pressure of his kiss and Cait fell into his warmth. As the cheers surrounding them broke into their kiss, Cait stumbled back. Turning, she bowed to the clapping crowd and laughed, playing the kiss off as showmanship.

Cait dashed from the floor. Throwing a glance over her shoulder, she saw Shane standing in the middle of the dance floor, his eyes offering as much of a threat as a promise. A shiver ran through Cait and she ducked beneath the pass-through of the bar, determined to return to normal.

"Aye, so you let that one kiss you but not me?" Patrick demanded, half-joking.

Cait poked him in the ribs and moved to take a drink order.

"He owns the place, after all," she called lightly. The bitter truth of it hit her though and she swallowed against the anger that rose in her throat. Why did Shane think that she couldn't afford the building? Was she just some charity case to him? Her mother's words rising in her head, Cait tried to shake off her feelings of insecurity.

"Hey, what's with you?" Aislinn called from the end of the bar. With a sigh, Cait went to her.

"Nothing, why?"

"Um, I can read your feelings? Duh?" Aislinn said and knocked her fingers against her head.

"Yeah, well I can read your thoughts. Should I take a peek at what you think of Dr. Hotness?" Cait said bitchily.

Brushing off Cait's comment, Aislinn reached out and touched her hand.

"What's wrong, honey? Why are you feeling insecure? The kiss?"

Cait shrugged her shoulder and glared across the room at Shane's back where he sat with Baird.

"Shane laughed at me when I said that I wanted to buy this building. And, well, I went to see my mom tonight. She pretty much echoed the same sentiment about me not being good enough for the rich folk." Cait shrugged her shoulders and wiped at a spill on the bar.

"Cait Gallagher, that is nonsense. You are just as good if not better than every person in this town. You have good heart, a solid reputation, and this business is wonderful. Just look around you!" Aislinn gestured to the full pub of happy people dancing and drinking. "You did this."

Cait smiled at her cousin's enthusiasm. "You're right. I did do this."

"And that makes you a badass woman."

"Yes. That makes me a badass woman," Cait agreed with a wicked smile on her face. Leaning over she kissed Aislinn's cheek.

"You're good for me, cousin. Now, go flirt with the good doctor," Cait instructed.

"I think that I am just going to go. Have to open the shop early and all," Aislinn said and averted her gaze.

Cait raised an eyebrow at her but only nodded. Cait watched as Aislinn stood and walked to the edge of the dance floor. Instead of going over to the table, she waved at the men and then hightailed it from the pub. Cait gasped as Baird jumped up and followed her. Oh, she so wished that she could run out on the street to see what would happen!

Shane cocked his head at her in a question but Cait turned from him. She needed to think about her reaction to him and now was not the time. Mechanically, Cait moved through the motions as the evening wound down.

"Last call," Cait called, checking her watch. Most of the crowd had dwindled anyway. Some of the pubs around town locked the doors at closing time, allowing patrons to stay longer but no longer serving new customers. Sometimes Cait did that but not this evening. She needed some time to think.

Cait smiled and settled tabs until she felt like her face would crack. Finally, she blew out a breath and made her way over to wipe off a bar table.

"Cait," Shane said from behind her and Cait jumped and turned.

"Oh, I thought everyone was out," Cait said. Her pulse jumped as she looked into Shane's eyes.

"They are. Patrick is doing dishes in the kitchen," Shane said.

Cait's stomach did a little twist and she watched Shane warily as he walked towards her, backing her up against the bar. Cait put her hands up on his chest lightly to stop him.

"Shane, stop."

"Why? I want you. Come home with me," Shane asked, his lips inches from hers. Cait's head swam as lust pooled low in her stomach. She felt so tiny pressed against the bar, Shane's muscular body pressing into hers. Gently, she eased back from his lips.

"No, not tonight. Not like this," Cait whispered.

"Not like what? It's clear that we want each other. We are both single, unattached adults," Shane said, his arms braced on either side of Cait.

"I know. But, I don't know. Perhaps it isn't best, you know, what with you owning the building that I work in and all that. Wouldn't want you to go slumming for an evening," Cait said and ducked under his arm. She jumped as he grabbed her arm and whipped her back to him.

"Slumming?" Shane asked dangerously.

"You know, having your fun with us poor people before you move on to something better," Cait said bitterly.

"I have no idea what you are talking about, Cait,"

Shane said. Cait met his eyes and wished that she would let herself read his mind.

"I'm sure that you wouldn't," Cait murmured and eased her arm from his hand. Shane threw up his hands and backed up from her.

"You are, quite possibly, the most infuriating woman. Hot, then cold, hot, then cold. Figure it out," Shane shouted and stomped from the bar.

Cait's pulse hammered and she took a deep breath against the twist of unease in her stomach. Every inch of her wanted to run after Shane. Instead, she hefted a tray of glasses and called for Patrick. There was work to finish.

CHAPTER 18

*C*AIT WOKE WITH a grumpiness that wasn't going to be shaken just by the cup of coffee that she brewed. Staring morosely into her empty fridge, she contemplated going for a full Irish somewhere. Cait wondered if she should go talk to Fiona about her mood. Shaking her head, she slammed the refrigerator door. What she needed was a nice healthy crying jag. Or a good long sulk. The problem was, Cait rarely allowed herself a crying jag or a good sulk. She'd cried more this week than she had in three years. Cait hated feeling moody. Perhaps cleaning her apartment would shake her mood, she thought as she eyed her small space.

Dismissing that idea, Cait thought about the one thing this week that had truly made her happy.

Smiling, she drank her cup of coffee and checked her watch. If she hustled, she'd have enough time to stop by the Donovans' for a surprise chat. Maybe she'd even get some insight into lasting relationships, Cait thought.

Pulling on a black tank and jeans, Cait tossed her messenger bag over her shoulder and hit the street, detouring down the road to the flower shop. Cait pulled sunglasses over her eyes to block the bright sunshine. Squinting, she saw Ellen, Shane's employee, leaning against a building talking into a cell phone. Ellen brought her hand up to cover her mouthpiece and Cait cocked her head at her. That was weird.

With zero shame, Cait reached out and scanned Ellen's mind.

"That idiot is clueless. I've got the books rigged and he thinks everything is fine. Just be sure to transfer the rest of the money by tomorrow and we'll get out of here. Let's go to London," Ellen said into the phone.

A white flash of heat hit her and, instantly enraged, Cait stormed down the street to grab Ellen's arm.

"Ouch, what are you doing?" Ellen shrieked. "Oh, it's you. I'm not sleeping with your man so you can back off." Ellen sneered at her and jerked her arm from Cait's hand. Cait stared at her open-mouthed.

"No but you're stealing from him," Cait hissed.

Ellen's face paled and she hit the button on her phone and shoved it in her pocket.

"You have no idea what you're talking about," Ellen said, straightening her shoulders.

"Don't I?" Cait blocked Ellen from moving past her. She barely registered that people were beginning to stop in the street to watch.

"I will not stand here and let you throw accusations at me," Ellen said.

"Oh, you aren't cooking the books?" Cait demanded.

"What are you talking about?" Ellen said.

"You and your little boyfriend. You're skimming the books. Planning to transfer money tonight?" Cait nodded towards the phone.

"You'd better back off," Ellen said and pushed Cait. Cait stumbled back a moment, in shock that Ellen had laid hands on her. A flash of rage ripped through her.

Cait saw red. Without thinking, she slammed Ellen back against the building and got in her face.

"Going to London, are you?" Cait whispered.

Ellen's face went white and her eyes opened in horror.

"There is no way you would know that," Ellen whispered.

"So it's true then," Cait said.

"What are you, some kind of freak?" Ellen shouted at Cait and shoved her hard. Cait stumbled back again, no match for the taller woman. Ellen eyed her with her fist raised and then turned from her.

"Stay away from me, you freak. So help me God if you say one word to jeopardize my life, I'm coming after you," Ellen shouted at her before stomping down the sidewalk.

Cait watched her go, shame flowing over her at being called a freak. Her chest rose as she struggled for breath. What had just happened? She never fought. Not physically at least. If anything, being a pub owner, Cait was always the peacemaker. Looking up, she saw a line of people on the sidewalk across the street.

"Did you get a good show, then?" Cait shouted at them. The crowd quickly dispersed, but Cait knew that the damage was done. The news that Cait and Ellen had gotten into a fight on the street would be all over town by noon. With a sigh, Cait decided against the flowers and went back to get her car. It wasn't like she was running from town, but now was a good time to leave the small village. Cait prayed that the Donovans were home.

CHAPTER 19

CAIT'S HANDS TREMBLED as she gripped the wheel on the drive out to the Donovans' house. She replayed the ugly scene with Ellen in her head.

Ellen had known that something was off about Cait. Perhaps she had heard rumors that Grace's Cove had a few mystical touches to the village, Cait thought. She tried to shake off the feeling of being called a freak and instead focused on how to tell Shane what she had discovered about his business manager.

If Cait went and told him, Shane would ask for proof. Cait had nothing to give and it would be her word against Ellen's. Would Shane believe her? Cait wondered if she could tell him about her ability or not. Remembering how he had dismissed her ambitions the night before, Cait slammed the door shut on that thought.

And yet... Cait pounded her fist on the steering wheel. She couldn't let Shane continue to get ripped off either. Her thoughts in a whirlwind, Cait pulled into the drive at the Donovans' cottage.

Getting out of her car, Cait stretched and took a deep breath, allowing the soft summer breeze to calm her down. The door cracked open and Mr. Donovan popped his head out.

"Ah, Cait, I hear you've been fighting on the streets this morning!" Mr. Donovan waved cheerfully and came out to greet her.

"Seriously? Already?" It never ceased to surprise Cait how quickly gossip traveled in their small village. She supposed she should be used to it by now.

"Now, Cait, this is exciting stuff here," Mr. Donovan joked and led her around the corner of the house to where Mrs. Donovan sat in the shade, enjoying the view of the water. Two dogs raced across the grass to sniff at Cait's feet. Automatically she reached down to pet them.

"Hi, Mrs. Donovan," Cait called and felt a warm rush of happiness go through her when the old woman's face lit up.

Cait took the seat next to Mrs. Donovan and Mr. Donovan rushed to bring another chair forward, eager to hear the gossip.

"Cait got herself into a fight this morning, dear," Mr. Donovan said. Mrs. Donovan raised an eyebrow at Cait.

"I did, at that," Cait said. She opened her mind to Mrs. Donovan.

"Well, I'm sure that she had it coming to her," Mrs. Donovan said.

Cait laughed and reached out to pat the old woman on the shoulder. "She did indeed."

"What did she say?" Mr. Donovan asked.

"She said that the other girl probably had it coming to her," Cait said.

"Well, of course she did. I've never known you to fight. Break up a fight, yes. Restore order, yes, but fight? Never," Mr. Donovan said briskly.

Cait leaned back in her chair and stretched her legs out, allowing the calmness of her surroundings to soak into her bones.

"I have a problem," Cait admitted.

"Tell us, we'd love to help you," Mr. Donovan said immediately. Mrs. Donovan gave a subtle nod with her head.

"I found out some information this morning. About Shane. And I didn't find it out in a normal way," Cait said, raising a finger to her head.

The Donovans watched her, waiting for her to go on.

"And, I…I think that I may have fallen for him." Cait raised her hands and let them drop back into her lap.

"Ah," Mr. Donovan said.

"I can't tell him about this information without telling him about my ability. I'm scared that he'll walk away from me," Cait said.

"How bad is this information? Is this what you were fighting about?" Mr. Donovan asked.

"It was and it's bad. It will hurt him and his business significantly," Cait said.

"Well, if you love him, you must tell him," Mrs. Donovan said.

"But I can't prove it. That's the problem," Cait protested.

"Does he love you?" Mr. Donovan asked.

"I suppose that is the question, isn't it?" Cait whispered.

"Is there any way that you can show him what he needs to know about his business without telling him about your ability? Gather proof?" Mr. Donovan asked.

Cait sat forward and thought about that. If she went to Galway and confronted Ellen, perhaps she could gather more information. Or, maybe she could gather some clues from the various people that lived in his investment properties. She'd be a detective!

"If I go to Galway, I bet that I could confront her and get what I need," Cait said.

"Tell him about you. Trust him to believe in you," Mrs. Donovan urged.

Cait sighed. "How? How can I trust him with this? What man would want to be with a freak like me?" Cait whispered, tears pricking her eyes.

"That's nonsense," Mr. Donovan said briskly. "I can tell you that after years of living with a woman, she can read your mind whether she has the ability to or not. You're a fine woman, Cait Gallagher, with a heart pure as sunlight."

Heat crept up Cait's cheeks and she couldn't help but smile at Mr. Donovan.

"He's right, Cait. Don't go to Galway. Tell him how you know. Trust him to believe in you. Give him the chance to believe in who you are," Mrs. Donovan urged.

"I don't know if I can do that yet," Cait said.

"It's true, what he says about relationships. When you love someone for so long, you fall into this rhythm of knowing who they are, what they want, and what they are thinking. You don't need to be a mind reader to know when they are mad at you or unhappy, you just feel it," Mrs. Donovan said.

"Look at how you have helped us. You're no freak. You're special," Mr. Donovan said.

"Well, thank you, and speaking of that, how can I help you both today?" Cait said, switching the subject. She needed some time to think.

Cait spent the next hour giving Mr. Donovan instructions on how to run the household, errands to do, and suggestions for Mrs. Donovan's medical care. Towards the end, she just acted as an interpreter for the couple, allowing them to laugh and enjoy a conversation about local gossip. When it came time for her to go, Cait could feel that her mood had lifted a bit.

Bending over, she pressed a kiss to Mrs. Donovan's papery cheek. The old woman clasped her arm.

"Tell him. Have faith in him," Mrs. Donovan urged.

"We'll see," Cait said.

"Will you come on Monday, still?"

"Of course, you can plan for it. I like being here," Cait said.

Mr. Donovan led her to her car. He stopped her before she got in and embraced her in a big bear hug. Cait allowed herself to relax into the hug and inhaled the scent of cigar and soap.

"You're a good girl, Cait. Shane would be lucky to have you," Mr. Donovan said.

"Thanks, Mr. D. That means a lot," Cait said.

Smiling, she backed out of their driveway and followed the road towards the village. She opened her windows to the ocean breeze. Should she tell Shane? Cait allowed the thought to circle her head all the way into town. Finally, she drew her car up in front of Shane's office, knowing that he was probably working today. Sitting in her car, she stared at his office for several minutes, her stomach in knots.

Could she just go in there and tell him that she had read Ellen's mind and that she was skimming the books on him? Cait clutched the wheel and a faint sheen of sweat broke out across her brow. The Donovans made it seem so easy. Paralyzed by fear, Cait drew in a deep breath before finally shifting her car out of park and down the lane.

Reaching for her cell phone, she called the pub.

"Patrick, can you handle the shifts today? Maybe call Annie in? I need the day off," Cait said into the phone as she passed the sign pointing towards Galway.

CHAPTER 20

CAIT GRIMACED AS she drove into Galway. She hated driving in bigger cities and though Galway wasn't as big as Dublin, Cait had grown used to the ebb and flow of small-town traffic. She swore as a car cut her off. Typical of the city.

Cait drove towards city centre, uncertain where to start. She wished that she had done a little more research prior to coming into the city. She knew that one of Shane's buildings rested right on the main square and planned to go there first to ask after Ellen. As a property manager, Ellen most likely lived in one of the apartment buildings that Shane owned.

Cait smiled as she drove into the square and admired the line of flags on one end and the people sitting in cafes along another. Galway was a fun city – a cross between small-town Ireland and big-city Dublin. If she had to pick, she'd rather spend time in Galway than Dublin. Spying a parking spot, Cait wrenched her wheel to the left and pulled in, waving a hand as angry horns sounded behind her.

Getting out of her car, Cait stretched and pulled her phone from her messenger bag to pull up the Google app. She knew that Shane had an apartment building right on the main square, but had forgotten the name of it. Cait leaned against her car as she did some sleuthing.

"Aha, of course he would name his building that." Cait rolled her eyes as she read her phone. The Baron was located just steps from where she had parked and Cait considered it a good sign. Cait straightened and tucked her phone in her back pocket. Her stomach twisted and she stopped to think about her approach. Did she know what she was doing? Cait shrugged her shoulder. She was used to improvising on the fly being a pub owner and she trusted her judgment to lead her in the right direction.

Cait followed the sidewalk down a small hill and came to stand in front of the Baron. Shane couldn't be faulted for his taste, Cait thought. A rustic brownstone of a building, the Baron had the charm of yesteryear mixed with the sleekness of modern windows and iron fixtures. Cheerful blooms spilled out of several window boxes and the front stoop was clean. Cait imagined that there was quite a wait-list to live in an apartment building such as this one.

The large double door opened and an elderly gentleman stepped out. The lines of his face sagged down and he stooped over the large box he was carrying. Instinctively, Cait ran up the steps to hold the door for him.

"Thank you, miss," the old man said tiredly.

"Hi, I'm Cait," Cait said impulsively.

The old man turned, his startling blue eyes lost in the wrinkles of his face, and he nodded at her. "Seamus."

"Can I help you?" Cait offered impulsively.

Seamus shrugged and motioned with his head towards a van parked in front that Cait had missed. The back doors were thrown open and an assortment of boxes, lamps and furniture were tucked in the back.

"Are you moving?" Cait asked and took one end of the box.

"I am, at that. Not by choice," Seamus huffed as they maneuvered the steps carefully before walking to the back of the van. Cait helped him to ease the box onto the floor of the van and then turned to examine Seamus' face more closely.

"Why? What happened?" Cait asked. She was tempted to read his mind but decided to let him speak first.

Seamus shrugged and pulled a small pipe from his pocket. He eased down on the back tailgate of the van and lit the pipe, puffing several times before exhaling a plume of smoke.

"I'm being forced out. Raised the rent," Seamus said.

"Shane raised the rent?" Cait questioned.

"You know Shane? Haven't seen him in half a year. No, Ellen did," Seamus said.

"Was it the typical yearly increase?" Cait asked. Her stomach twisted even further into knots.

"It certainly was not! I was astounded. I've been here for years and never seen such a price hike as this one," Seamus said angrily.

"How much did she raise it?"

"Two hundred euros more a month!" Seamus exclaimed.

"What? That's madness," Cait said, just as angry as Seamus was. With every fiber of her being she knew that Shane had not authorized the rent increases.

"I can't afford that. I'm retired and have a budget. I…I love this place though. Breaks my heart to leave it. I feel like I am still alive living here. I can walk to the pub, meet up with friends for lunch, or get my daily shopping done. If I have to move out of the city I'll be dependent on public transportation. I don't want to give up this life," Seamus said and Cait caught a glimpse of tears in his eyes.

"Seamus, look at me," Cait said. The old man turned and met her eyes. Cait reached out and put her hand on his arm.

"I will make this right. Don't pack anything else, okay? Go grab a pint and I'll have this fixed by the end of the day. I promise," Cait said.

Seamus' eyes lit up.

"Can you really do that?"

"I can. I'm good friends with Shane. I'll make it right. Here's my phone number and all of my information," Cait said as she recited her personal information and watched the old man write it on a small notebook he pulled from his coat. "But, I'll need your help."

"Anything at all," Seamus said as he stood up and straightened his shoulders proudly.

"I'm going after Ellen. Do you know where she lives? I suspect that we won't be able to find her after today," Cait said.

"I do, actually. I fixed some wiring in her apartment a few months back. I used to be an electrician," Seamus said.

"Perfect," Cait said.

"She manages and lives in one of the other buildings. It's off the square, down towards the water. A lovely building as well, but I like this location better," Seamus said and rattled off the address for Cait.

"Thank you, Seamus. Now, I just have to figure out how to get in," Cait murmured.

"Ah, that I can help you with. I still have the building key as Ellen wanted me to come back for another apartment." Seamus smiled cagily.

Cait leaned down and kissed the old man's cheek enthusiastically.

"Can I borrow it or do you want to come with?"

"Wouldn't miss this for the world. She's a nasty one," Seamus said.

Cait smiled at him and waited for Seamus to close up his van. It looked like she had gotten herself a sidekick.

CHAPTER 21

"So, SHE'S STEALING from Shane, isn't she?" Seamus said as he strapped himself into Cait's car. Cait nodded at him and glanced over her shoulder before jutting the car into traffic.

"She is at that. Though I hadn't realized how much," Cait said.

"She owes me almost a thousand euros then," Seamus said as he shifted in his seat and gestured towards a street for Cait to turn on.

"We'll get it for you. I promise," Cait said.

Cait jumped as her phone buzzed in her back pocket. Keeping an eye on the road, she shifted to one side and pulled the phone out, groaning at the name on the display.

"Who is it?" Seamus asked.

"Shane," Cait said. She silenced the phone and put it on her lap.

"Aren't you going to tell him what is going on?"

"It's complicated," Cait said.

"Doesn't seem that complicated to me. It's his business, isn't it?" Seamus said.

Cait nodded and kept her eyes on the road while a million thoughts ran through her head. Shane rarely called her. He must have heard about the fight and was probably calling to yell at her. Determined to see this through, Cait ignored the message indicator on her phone and steered her car to a stop in front of a large, sleek building by the waterfront.

A far cry from the Baron, this building was all glass and sleek metal lines. Cait could see the appeal as the views of the water had to be wonderful. She suspected that she would be happier in the Baron though if she had to pick.

"Yuppie building," Seamus muttered as he got out of the car.

Cait looked both ways before weaving them both through the busy traffic that ringed the street.

Seamus led the way up the steps to a glass sliding door. Pulling his keys from his pocket, he picked through the ring until he found the one he was looking for. Slipping it in the lock, he eased the door quietly open and motioned for Cait to step into the cool lobby.

Here, white was the dominant theme. White walls, a low white couch and a white side table comprised the medium-sized lobby. A white panel of mailboxes and stainless-steel elevator doors took up much of the wall to the left. Seamus gestured towards the elevator doors and pressed the up button.

Cait felt a sheen of sweat break out on her forehead

and she tried to stay still as they quietly waited for the elevator.

"Do you have a plan?" Seamus said.

"Nope," Cait admitted.

"Ah, well. Probably better," Seamus said easily and surprised a laugh from Cait. She swung her arm over his shoulders.

"I'm glad you're here. Um, just, listen, if some weird stuff goes down…don't judge me too hard, okay?" Cait asked.

Seamus turned his bright eyes on Cait.

"I've seen a lot of weird in my life. I can't imagine you'll surprise me too much. Just don't kill anyone," Seamus said.

"That I won't. I'm really not the violent sort." Cait smiled at the old man and they stepped into the elevator together.

Cait stared at the silver doors as they whooshed closed in front of them. Taking a few deep breaths, she tried to steady herself.

"Ellen's got the penthouse, naturally. Which doesn't make sense to me as Shane could make more money if he rented it out. I suppose it is probably part of her salary," Seamus said.

"I'm sure she negotiated every last thing she could from Shane," Cait murmured.

"Is Shane your boyfriend?" Seamus asked.

"It's complicated," Cait said again and stepped into the hall as the elevator doors opened on the top floor. Cool gray tones were prevalent here. A darker gray carpet lined the hall and complemented the dove gray of the paint color. A large white door was the only door in the hallway. Taking a breath, Cait stepped up and put her finger over the peephole.

"Ready?"

"Let's get her, girl," Seamus whispered. Cait knocked briskly on the door and heard voices stop talking and then the sound of soft footsteps approaching the door. Cait knew that she was peering through the peephole. She dropped her shields and reached out with her mind.

Who is at the door? Why can't I see out? Ellen thought.

Cait knocked again and reached out further, finding another mind to read further in the apartment. This must be Jason, the boyfriend, Cait thought as she scanned his mind and realized that he was shoving money into a duffel bag.

Open the door, you bitch, Cait thought and waited until she could read that Ellen had decided to open the door. With a soft click, the lock slid open and before Ellen could open the door, Cait moved.

She turned the knob and slammed the door into the room, hitting Ellen in the head and rushing into the apartment, Seamus quick on her heels.

"What the hell!" Ellen screamed.

A man ran into the room and stopped, staring in confusion at Cait and Seamus. This must be Jason, Cait thought. Tall, ripped, and blond, he was a good match for Ellen's beauty.

The door opened up into the main living space. It was a contemporary condo with a compact kitchen that lined one wall and a marble breakfast bar that separated the eating area from the living area. A wide expanse of windows offered a view of the harbor and Cait could imagine curling up before the windows with a cup of tea and a good book. A separate hallway led away from the room presumably to a bathroom or a bedroom, Cait thought. Jason had come from there.

Boxes covered every available surface in the room. Walls were bare, lamps stood next to boxes with their cords wrapped around the bases, and a pile of shoes lay next to a large suitcase.

"Going somewhere?" Cait said as she moved away from the door and into the kitchen, putting the breakfast bar between her and Ellen. Seamus followed suit, staying a step behind her, a rotund, angry sidekick.

"Who is this?" Jason gestured to Cait.

"She's some freak that has a crush on Shane," Ellen said and rubbed her forehead. Cait derived a distinct level of satisfaction from the fact that there was a blaring red welt forming on her perfect skin.

"Why is Seamus here?" Jason said.

"Hi, guys!" Seamus said cheerfully.

"Seamus, you need to leave before I have you evicted," Ellen said fiercely.

"Ah, I don't know about that. Seems as though it's best that I stay here with Cait," Seamus said easily.

"You don't know what you are talking about. I'm your landlord. She's just…a freak of nature," Ellen said and moved into the kitchen.

"Don't try to change the subject," Cait said and gestured around the room. "Does Shane know that you are leaving?" Cait raised an eyebrow at Ellen.

"Of course he does," Ellen said. Cait reached out and scanned her mind.

Shit, shit, shit. We were so close to getting out. We need to get the money that is in the bag in the living room and in the bedroom. Hide the evidence. Then we can go, Ellen thought.

Cait turned and scanned the room, looking for a duffel bag. She found it sitting next to the suitcase of shoes, a non-descript black duffel bag.

"That's a lie, Ellen," Cait said smoothly as she eased herself slowly around the counter.

"Get out before I make Jason force you to leave," Ellen said softly.

"Is that a threat?" Cait turned and eyed Jason. "You going to toss me out, big boy?"

Why did I get involved in this? I should just go be with Mary. She's easy to be with, Jason thought. Cait smiled widely at him.

"I don't think that Jason is going to do anything," Cait said.

Moving quickly, she ran to the duffel bag and snatched it up, running back to the kitchen to stand by Seamus.

"So help me God, if you open that I will throw you from this window," Ellen said, her voice low and just a bit crazy.

"Aye? You want to add murder to embezzling?" Cait asked and drew the zipper down on the bag.

"Holy…" Seamus whispered as stacks of euros tumbled onto the counter.

"Seamus, why don't you count out your thousand that she owes you," Cait said. She braced her hands on the counter, her heart pounding. "The jig's up, Ellen. Turn yourself in."

"Like hell I will. Jason and I have a flight to London tonight. We're going to start a whole new life and get the hell away from this dumpy country," Ellen seethed and moved towards the breakfast bar. "Jason, get rid of them."

Jason moved forward and hesitated on the other side of the breakfast bar.

"What are you going to do, Jason?" Cait taunted him.

"Um, you are going to have to leave," Jason said.

"Try it," Seamus said easily and Cait laughed as the old man pulled out a pocketknife.

"Am I? I don't think so. Your girlfriend here is going to call Shane and turn herself in," Cait said.

"This is ridiculous, Jason. You are going to let an old man brandish a toothpick of a knife at you and you're not doing anything? Seriously!" Ellen fumed and moved closer.

"Listen, Ellen, I didn't sign up to hurt anyone," Jason began. Ellen cut him off.

"Stop being such a weakling. Do something!" Ellen shrieked at him, the veins in her neck standing out unattractively.

Jason took a step closer and Seamus held up his knife.

"It may be small but I've gutted many a fish in one swipe with it. I imagine gutting a man is much the same," Seamus threatened. Cait felt her heart soar at the old man's gumption.

"Here's what's going to happen, Ellen. You're going to confess to Shane and do your time and hopefully, many years from now, you'll start a new life far away from all of this," Cait said carefully.

"Nice try, you freak. Jason, get the bag from them," Ellen demanded.

Cait grabbed the bag from the counter and upended the stacks of cash all over the floor.

"Oops," Cait said and smiled as Ellen began to wheeze.

"Jason, get the other bag. Forget this crap. We have more than enough to start over," Ellen instructed. Jason hesitated and Cait pounced.

"Bet you'd rather be with Mary," Cait said demurely. Jason's eyes widened in surprise and Ellen whipped her head around to stare at Jason.

"Mary? Mary! You've been seeing that bitch behind my back?" Ellen shrieked.

"What? No, I mean, maybe a little. Shit, how would she know that?" Jason said.

"You have? I knew it. I knew it! Lord knows what you see in that mousey woman," Ellen shouted.

"Well, she probably doesn't live a life of crime, so, you know, that's a point in her favor," Cait said mildly.

"And you...you freak. What is it? Can you read minds? How do you know this?"

"It doesn't matter how I know it," Cait said.

"Bullshit. You're a stupid freak from small-town Grace's Cove. I'd always heard that place was cursed and everyone in it was weird. Now, I know the truth," Ellen said. Cait felt heat creep up her cheeks. She jutted her chin out as both Jason and Seamus turned to eye her warily.

"Listen very carefully, Ellen. You are going to confess to Shane or I will ruin you. Do you understand that?"

"I'd like to see you try," Ellen scoffed.

Cait sighed and reached out to dig into the far corners of Ellen's mind.

"I know that you plan to ditch Jason once you get to London because your man...Heath, is it? Yes, Heath lives there. I know that you have stashed another 10,000 euros in a separate account under your mother's maiden name of Murphy. Your boobs are fake, you used to be fat, and you have always thought that you were better than everyone else and deserved a better life. Yet, you've never managed to marry into a rich circle, have you?" Cait said softly as she circled the counter, keeping her eyes on Ellen. "Your family wants nothing to do with you and you have no real friends as your only focus is on yourself. You can't even manage to keep your violet plant alive."

Ellen drew in a deep breath as her face flushed with shame. She stood there, looking like a fish out of water, as her mouth struggled to form a sentence.

"Heath? What the hell, Ellen?" Jason shouted at her.

"I...I," Ellen gasped. Jason whirled away from her and grabbed a coat from the counter.

"I'm done with you. I'm done with this. You can get in trouble on your own. I never asked for this. I want a nice, easy life. And yes, I've been seeing Mary and she's twice the woman you are," Jason shouted in Ellen's face. He moved past her towards the door. Ellen's face turned ugly.

"You'll never get good sex from her. Have a nice, mediocre life," Ellen shouted at Jason's back. Jason stopped short at the open door and the people that blocked his way.

Cait felt her heart drop into her stomach and she bowed her head, wondering just how much he'd heard.

"Am I interrupting something?" Shane asked from the door, two guards standing behind him. Ellen froze for a moment before turning a charming smile on Shane.

"Thank you so much for coming, especially with the Gardai. These...people have broken into my apartment." Ellen sniffed at Cait and Seamus.

Cait rolled her eyes. If Shane believed Ellen's act then she would really need to reconsider if she was in love with this man.

Shane's eyes tracked the room before meeting Cait's. Cait held his gaze steadily.

"Is that so? Cait, is the pub not prospering? Resorting to breaking and entering these days?" Shane asked. Cait blew out a breath that she hadn't realized that she had been holding and smiled lightly at him.

"Well, you know, I like to live on the edge," Cait said.

"You are just going to stand here and allow this?" Ellen demanded and Cait whirled around to face her.

"Oh give it up. He came here with the guards. You're busted!"

The Guardai moved past Shane and towards Ellen. Ellen backed up into Jason.

"It was all Jason, I swear," Ellen said, throwing Jason directly in the line of fire. Jason backed up and scoffed down at her, his mouth hanging open.

"It wasn't," Cait offered and smiled at the glare that Ellen sliced her way.

"Aye, so I heard," Shane said and Cait felt her stomach plummet. So, he had been listening. She gulped as a lump filled her throat and tears pricked her eyes. This was to be it, then. There was no way he'd be interested in her now.

"Ellen, you're being charged with embezzlement." One of the guards began to read Ellen her rights as he clasped the handcuffs around her wrists.

Ellen whirled around and stared at Cait.

"Thanks a lot, you stupid freak. Go back to your little town and do your magick or whatever the shit it is you can do. Stay away from me," Ellen hissed at her. Cait could only look at the floor as Ellen was dragged from the room, professing her innocence the entire time.

"Jason, did you have a part in this?" Shane asked.

"I, yes, I did. But not in the way you think. I told her that it was wrong and that I wanted no part of it. Listen, I've got another girl. A good girl with a good heart. I never should have been caught up in this. I'm sorry. I wish you no harm, truly. Sorry, Seamus," Jason said and gestured to the old man.

"What did you do to Seamus?" Shane asked, surprise evident in his voice.

"Um, Ellen raised his rent," Jason said.

"Is that true, Seamus? Why didn't you tell me?" Shane demanded, looking hurt.

"Aye, I thought it was on your orders." Seamus shrugged. "I was moving me stuff out today."

"Well, move it back in. You aren't going anywhere," Shane said.

"You're a good man, Shane." Seamus smiled.

Shane turned to Jason and studied him carefully.

"If I don't press charges against you, do I have your word that you will settle down and lead a normal life?" Shane asked.

"You have my word. I only want things to be easy," Jason said gratefully.

"Then go." Shane gestured to the door and Jason lost no time in seeing himself out.

"Well, now that that is taken care of, I'm going to take Seamus home," Cait said quickly and moved past the counter, her feet hitting stacks of cash. "Oh, and, uh, here is a bunch of money. There is more in the black duffel bag in the bedroom."

"Cait, wait." Shane moved to stand in front of her.

Cait's stomach twisted and she straightened her shoulders. Unable to meet his eyes, she looked over his shoulder.

"We need to talk about this. I'm grateful for your help, though I don't know how you ended up here," Shane said.

"How did you figure it out?" Cait demanded.

"I found enough discrepancies in the books that I figured out where it was coming from. But, I came today because I heard that you'd had a fight on the street. You never fight with anyone so I figured you found out. Not sure how, though." Shane tilted his head at her.

"Ah, well, all is well then. I've got to get going," Cait said nervously and turned to gesture to Seamus.

"Come on, Seamus, let's get you home," Cait said quickly.

Once again, she turned her back on Shane.

"One of these days you'll quit walking away from me, Cait Gallagher," Shane called after her. Cait shivered at the promise his words held.

CHAPTER 22

"WHEN ARE YOU going to tell him that you can read minds?" Seamus asked easily once they were back in the car. Cait's foot slipped off the pedal and she glanced quickly at Seamus.

"So, figured that one out, did you?"

"It was fairly obvious," Seamus said.

"I can't tell him. What man wants to live with that?" Cait asked.

"I think he'd be right lucky to have you, Cait," Seamus said.

Cait just shrugged her shoulders and kept her eyes on the road. Spotting a parking space in front of the Baron, she eased the car in.

"Come in for a quick pint?"

"Sure, I'll help you take a few boxes in as well," Cait said.

Seamus stopped before getting out of the car.

"Cait, you need to talk to Shane. Look at what you did for him. You could have been hurt! You have to know that he would love anyone who would put themselves on the line for him like that," Seamus said.

"Yeah, well, you know…just trying to do a good deed," Cait said.

"He loves you. It was all over his face. Trust this old man," Seamus said wisely. Cait gaped after him as he stepped from the car.

"Well, he loves the me that he thinks he knows," Cait said stubbornly from across the top of the car.

"So? Give the man a chance to love all of you," Seamus said and gestured up the stairs to his apartment. A heaviness hit her chest and her mother's words filled her head. Cait didn't think that she would ever be able to truly show herself to Shane. She looked at the old man's bright eyes and a wave of courage hit her. Why couldn't she tell him? Maybe it was far past the time to show the world who she was, Cait thought. With a wide smile she looped her arm through Seamus' arm.

"Let's have that pint, shall we?"

CHAPTER 23

*C*AIT WALKED DOWN the steps from Seamus' apartment with a lighter heart. She'd spent an enjoyable hour with the old man while he had teased her about her ability and asked her if she could give him the winning lottery numbers. It was nice to be treated normally and even to poke some fun at her gift. Fun, Cait thought. She needed more fun in her life. Lately it had been all intensity and angst.

She let herself out the front door of the Baron and stopped short to see Shane leaning on her car.

"Shane."

"Cait, I just stopped by to have a word with Seamus and saw your car here. I figured that I would wait," Shane said.

"You could have come up. We were just having a pint." Cait shrugged a shoulder awkwardly.

"Walk with me?" Shane gestured to the square.

Helpless not to go with him, Cait nodded and walked by his side silently.

Shane didn't touch her. Together, they crossed the street in silence. Cait stared at the gray cobblestones of the square and felt a sense of dread fill her. They walked quietly for a few moments.

"I just came from talking to Ellen," Shane began.

Cait felt her heartbeat pick up and a thin layer of sweat kissed her forehead.

"She had some interesting things to say about you."

"Is that so?" Cait asked.

"Is it true?"

"Is what true, Shane?" Cait asked stubbornly, forcing Shane to say it.

"Can you read minds?"

Cait let out a small breath. The time had finally come. She could no longer hide behind her own expectations or boundaries.

"Yes."

One word, said so simply, and yet it had the power to change everything, Cait thought. She couldn't bring herself to look at Shane. A sheen of tears coated her eyes and she blinked furiously against them, refusing to cry in front of Shane. Instead, Cait watched a young couple laugh and dance through the square together. She wanted to be that couple…light and carefree.

"When were you going to tell me?" Shane's words carried a hint of anger and Cait turned to face him.

"Was I supposed to tell you?" Cait asked, tilting her head to look into his gorgeous face. By God, he was angry, Cait thought in surprise.

"You didn't think that that was a valuable piece of information for me to have?"

"I didn't think that it was any of your business," Cait said and jutted her chin out.

Shane's face darkened and he struggled to breathe. Cait watched in fascination as he quelled his anger.

"That's a fairly important thing to tell the person who wants to be with you," Shane finally said.

A fissure of anger worked its way through Cait. She took a deep breath and thought...*nice voice, use your nice voice*.

"Oh? You want to be with me? In what way? As your sidepiece? As a fun-when-you-want-it kind of girl?"

"What? No, I never said that," Shane said and grabbed her arm. Cait wrenched it away.

"Yeah, well you didn't say a lot, did you?"

"Well, apparently I didn't have to as you can just read my mind!" Shane shouted at her.

Cait stopped and stared at him and a cold rage filled her.

"I have never read your mind. Ever. I have morals, you know," Cait whispered furiously, offended to her very core.

"Oh, so you can just turn it off and on? How was I supposed to know as YOU NEVER TOLD ME!" Shane shouted, betrayal lacing his face.

"Why? So you could add it to the list of things that make me unsuitable for you?" Cait demanded, her hands at her hips. Her whole body trembled with anger. She couldn't believe that they were doing this, in public at the square. She could see people steering clear of them and Cait could only imagine the picture they made. She was surprised to find that she was beyond caring.

"What are you talking about? Why wouldn't you suit me?" Shane said as he squinted at her in confusion.

Cait felt it build in her, all her insecurities, her mother's words, her sadness, and unable to stop herself she shrieked at Shane:

"Because I'm not good enough! You made that clear when you laughed at my dream of buying the pub. You only date people who are rich and from out of town. You buy the nicest things, have the best house in town, and only drive the fanciest cars. I'm not rich. I don't come from a stable upbringing. I'll never be on your level, Shane, so just leave me alone. Stop toying with my heart when you never meant to be with me anyway," Cait said, the steam going out of her words and trickling down into a whisper.

Shane gaped at her, his mouth struggling furiously to form words.

Cait held up her hand. "Just don't."

"You lied to me!" Shane said. "Don't try to change the subject to some stuff that isn't true and doesn't matter. Let's not forget the fact that you lied to me. You betrayed *me*, Cait," Shane said.

Cait's body trembled and she stared at Shane's furious face. He had completely dismissed her claims that she wasn't good enough as if they didn't matter. She didn't know if that meant that he didn't believe them or if he felt like her feelings weren't important. Confused, and not sure what to say next, Cait just stared at him helplessly.

Shane's phone rang and he raised his finger to her. Glancing at the phone, Cait could see his debate about answering. Reaching out, she scanned his mind.

"Go on, answer it, it's the Guardai."

Shane shot a shocked look at her.

"See? That's me, Shane. You'll never be able to change that," Cait said bitterly.

Shane just looked at her and shaking his head, he answered the phone. With one last look over his shoulder, he walked away from Cait, breaking her heart with every footstep.

Cait turned blindly and ran for her car, narrowly missing getting hit by cars as she raced across the street.

She'd been right all along, Cait thought, and hopping in her car, she raced from Galway, leaving her heart behind.

On the road, Cait picked up her phone and dialed Patrick.

"Hiya, Cait," Patrick answered cheerfully.

"Close the pub," Cait whispered.

"What's that?"

"I said, close the pub. Until further notice. I'll give you two weeks' pay," Cait said.

"Cait, what's wrong? You can't just close the pub!" Patrick's voice was filled with worry.

"I am. I'm sorry, Patrick. I'll let you know if anything changes," Cait said and hung up.

CHAPTER 24

S HANE TURNED FROM his phone call to find Cait
gone. He raced across the square to see that her
car no longer sat in its spot.

"Damn it," Shane said.

Frustrated, he stood on the sidewalk, unsure what to do
next. Fear and misery raced through him. He couldn't
believe it when Ellen had insisted that Cait could read
minds. But, it made sense especially as he had overheard
the last part of what Cait had said to Ellen in the penthouse. He felt like he'd been hit with a frying pan in the
face. Everything that he thought he knew about Cait had
shifted. A bitter taste of betrayal filled his mouth.

How could she think that she wasn't good enough?
Shane had always been kind to her and everyone else in
the village. Just because he liked nice things didn't mean
that he felt he was better than anyone. Shane enjoyed
spending the money he made from his hard work. Was that
a bad thing?

Shane sighed as he eyed the door to the Baron. He

needed to talk to Seamus and had to go back and finish pressing charges against Ellen. His heart heavy, he walked up the steps and knocked on the old man's door.

"Aye, Shane, good to see you," Seamus said as he opened the door and smiled widely at him. Shane felt a twinge of remorse at knowing what the old man had gone through.

"I wanted to stop by and tell you that you are welcome to stay here and that I'd like to offer you the rest of the year for free," Shane said quietly.

Seamus' eyes lit up, but then he examined Shane's face more closely.

"Why don't you come in for a moment?"

Shane nodded and stepped into the apartment, noting the piles of boxes that ranged the long wall of windows that looked out over the square. Regret filled him.

"I'm so sorry about this. I wish that you had contacted me," Shane said bitterly.

Seamus gestured him to a loveseat and offered him a bottle of Harp. Shane took it gratefully and Seamus pulled up a chair across from him.

"Ah, well, no harm done. If anything, it got me to do a nice deep clean," Seamus said cheerfully.

Shane winced at the ease with which the old man forgave him.

"Just like that? You aren't mad at me?" Shane asked.

"Now why would I be mad at you? It's that Ellen that's a witch after all," Seamus said, taking a long pull from his bottle of beer.

"Thank you," Shane said softly, staring at the floor.

"Ah, if you don't mind me saying, you look pretty

upset," Seamus said. "Did Ellen do more harm than you realized?"

"I'm still finding out just how much she took. I need to get back to the guards and see what else she has confessed to. I have my assistant calling every tenant we've had in order to make sure that everyone gets their money back," Shane said wearily.

"You'll figure it out," Seamus said.

"Yeah," Shane said quietly.

Seamus cleared his throat and allowed Shane to sit in silence for a moment. Finally, the old man gestured with his bottle.

"That Cait, she's a fine woman, isn't she?"

Shane nodded.

"Risked a lot for her to come up here like she did," Seamus continued.

Shane nodded again.

"She must really care about you," Seamus said.

Shane glared at the old man and Seamus laughed.

"Got it bad, do you?"

"She lied to me!" Shane burst out.

Seamus raised an eyebrow at Shane and gestured with his beer bottle for him to go on.

"I feel like I don't even know her. What else is she lying about?" Shane said.

"Well, now, it seems to me like a woman honorable enough to come up to Galway and try to save your business probably isn't hiding much."

"Yeah, that you know of," Shane said bitterly.

"Have you thought about it from her perspective? It isn't the easiest thing to reveal to someone," Seamus said.

"She should have told me," Shane insisted.

"Maybe. Maybe not. It's not something she can change. And, she would have been shunned by many if she had opened up about it," Seamus said.

Shane stopped and thought about it for a moment. He supposed that having to tell the world that you are different was probably pretty scary.

"Still…I'm not everyone. Things are different with me," Shane insisted.

"How so?"

"Well, I want more from her. I want to be with her! You are supposed to tell that to the person who wants to be with you," Shane said.

"Be with her? In what way?"

"Well…I," Shane said and stopped.

"Ah. I see. Have you told her that you love her?" Seamus said and took another sip of his beer.

"I haven't, actually," Shane whispered.

"So, you expect her to lay it all on the line for you but you haven't done the same for her?"

Annoyance sprang through Shane at the old man's words. It wasn't like that…was it?

"It's not like that," Shane said.

"Seems to me that you expect a lot of her but aren't doing the same yourself," Seamus said snippily.

"She said that she isn't good enough for my rich life-style," Shane said. "How does that even make sense?'

Seamus smiled and gestured to his apartment. "Well, there will always be class differences. Owners and employees, landlords and tenants. It's a power struggle. The one with less power will always feel more insecure."

Shane felt like someone had pulled the curtains back in his mind and sunshine flooded in.

"So, it's my job to make her feel secure," Shane said.

"Bravo, my boy. You haven't even told her you love her. How is *she* supposed to believe in *you*?"

"God, you're right. A hundred times, right. I've been so stupid."

"So? Fix it." Seamus smiled at him.

"I will. Hey, want a job? I'm looking for a new apartment manager," Shane said and Seamus' eyes lit up.

"Looks to me like this is the beginning of a new partnership, my friend," Seamus said and leaned over to tap his bottle against Shane's.

CHAPTER 25

*C*AIT RAN A BRUSH down the flank of one of Flynn's horses. Taking a deep breath of the stable scents, she pressed her cheek against the horse for a moment.

God, she'd been nothing but a crying wreck for three days now, Cait thought. She'd never been one to be so weepy and now she wondered just what it was she cried for. Was it the death of a relationship that she'd never really had? Or was it that she was saying goodbye to the boundaries that she had so carefully erected for herself and trying to step into her power as a grown woman?

Stepping back, she fed the horse a carrot before quietly leaving the stall. Keelin and Flynn had decided to extend their honeymoon and had been kind enough to lend her their house for the week, though Keelin had made Cait promise that she would spill all of the details when Keelin returned. Cait didn't know how long she planned to stay away from the village, she just wasn't ready to go back to the pub and put on a happy face for customers.

Cait knew the gossip in town. Rumors ran rampant about the closing of Gallagher's pub. Some suspected that it had to do with her fight with Ellen and that Shane had closed the building. Others thought that she wasn't paying her bills. Cait had gotten all of the gossip when she had called the Donovans to tell them that she couldn't make her Monday appointment.

Cait shrugged. She was past caring what people thought about her. What mattered was what she thought about herself. The problem was, she didn't know where she stood on that end.

Cait heard the yips of the dogs and looked up as Fiona approached her over the hills, carrying a basket in her arms.

"I thought that you'd like some pampering. I don't suppose you are feeding yourself well," Fiona said sternly.

Cait just shrugged her shoulders. She motioned for Fiona to come to the long deck that wrapped the large house. Grace's Cove was featured predominantly in the view. Cait hadn't sat here yet as she didn't want to think about her meeting with Grace. She wondered if Grace was watching her. Cait supposed that she was letting the mighty pirate queen down.

"This is a lovely spot," Fiona observed as she unpacked her basket on the long wooden table. A tureen of soup, warm brown bread, and a basket of fruit, along with plates, silverware, and a jug of apple cider.

"That's a lot of food," Cait said.

"Comfort food," Fiona said simply and ladled chunky vegetable soup into a bowl before passing it to Cait. She pulled out a crock of Irish butter, prepared two pieces of bread, and slid the plate to Cait. "Eat."

There was no arguing with Fiona's tone and Cait was surprised to feel a little rumble in her stomach as she looked down at the food. It was true; she'd barely eaten the past few days. Her appetite seemed to have disappeared.

Cait dutifully picked up the spoon and took her first bite of the soup. She moaned a little as the warm flavors that tasted like home filled her mouth. Suddenly ravenous, she gulped down a few more bites before grabbing for the bread. Grateful that Fiona said nothing, Cait concentrated on slowing her pace and allowing the food to settle.

"I went to see Sarah yesterday," Fiona said.

Cait paused with her bread halfway to her mouth.

"You did?"

"I did. Your mother is very sick, you know," Fiona said.

"She seems fine to me," Cait said. Fine enough to constantly criticize me, she thought.

"Aye, her physical health is fine. Her mental health… not so good. I found her eating a can of cat food," Fiona said quietly.

Cait stilled her hands as she felt a deep-rooted sadness fill her. Sadness for the woman her mother must have once been and grief for the fact that she would never be able to mend their relationship now.

"I…I suppose it is time to look into special care for her," Cait said. She mentally calculated the cost of doing so and shivered at the thought of the added expenses. Cait honestly didn't even know what her mother's financial situation was. Sarah had never shared that with her.

"There's a lovely assisted-housing spot in Shannon. Affordable, too," Fiona said. "I took the liberty of calling for you and I wrote down all of the information." Fiona slid a packet of papers to Cait.

"Thank you," Cait said, looking dully down at the packet of papers.

"What was she like before me? Did I really ruin her life?" Cait said impulsively.

Fiona leaned back, her eyebrows raised.

"Is that what you think, dear girl?"

"It's what I've been told," Cait said bitterly.

"Ah," Fiona said quietly. She picked up her cider and seemed to mull over her words carefully.

"Ah, is right. It's not a secret that we've had a hard relationship."

"No, it's not. And, I'm sorry for that. I've done what I can to pick up the slack. But, I would hardly say that you ruined her life. Sarah has always been a bitter, unhappy woman. Becoming a mother did little to change that in her."

Cait felt her heart grow a little lighter. So, perhaps she wasn't the reason for her mother's bitterness after all.

"Really?"

"Oh my, yes. She had very few friends. Typically she had nasty things to say about most people in town. She's only grown more reclusive over the years. Frankly, it's a miracle that you turned out as well as you did," Fiona said briskly.

Cait's cheeks flushed and she blinked as tears pricked her eyes.

"I don't think that I'm doing so well," Cait whispered.

"You're doing just fine, Cait Gallagher. You're a fine business owner, a loyal friend, and you're an old soul. You should be proud of yourself," Fiona said.

Cait raised one shoulder slightly and pursed her lips.

"You can't tell me that one man has taken all of your confidence? Where is my sassy, full-of-life Cait?" Fiona said worriedly.

Cait just shrugged. "I guess that I am trying to figure that out."

"Nobody's approval defines who you are, Cait. Not your mother's and certainly not a man's. You have to stand for yourself first," Fiona said softly.

"I'm trying…it's just…" Cait tore a piece of bread to pieces on her plate. "It's just that my mother thinks that my ability is the gift of the devil. She looked at me in complete disgust. That bitch of a woman Ellen called me a freak. And then, I finally told Shane about me and…he walked away. Said that I lied to him." Cait hiccupped out a small sob.

"It's been a tough week," Fiona said, gesturing with her spoon.

Cait was surprised to find that she could laugh.

"It has at that," Cait admitted.

"Well, from where I am sitting, I see a beautiful woman both inside and out. Your gift doesn't make you a freak. It makes you powerful beyond words. Don't let anyone else define what that means to you," Fiona said fiercely.

Cait smiled for the first time in days as a sense of power snuck through her.

"You've dealt with this...this whole being different thing," Cait observed.

"Aye, my whole life. I struggled with the same things that you did. But once I decided to step into my own power, nothing else mattered. People fell in line or they didn't. The ones that mattered, they stayed by me. The ones that didn't, shunned me. I'm forever grateful that I stopped hiding from myself. It has led to immeasurable happiness. Finding love after that only heightened it for me," Fiona said.

"Shane might be right. I didn't just betray him, I betrayed myself. I couldn't tell him honestly what I was," Cait said.

"Well, Shane has some growing up to do himself. It sounds like he expects an awful lot from you but I don't see him rolling out the red carpet for you around town," Fiona said huffily.

Cait eyed her.

"Keelin told me that you didn't like Shane. Why is that?"

"I didn't like him for her," Fiona amended.

"Do you for me?" Cait demanded.

"Only you can answer that." Fiona smiled wickedly at Cait and Cait laughed.

"Now, how long are you going to lick your wounds here?" Fiona asked.

"I don't feel right operating a business in Shane's building that he owns. I'll need to look around for a new spot, I think," Cait said.

"That's nonsense, Cait Gallagher. Business is business. You need to open up your bar and host a big party is what I think. Show the world that you don't care," Fiona suggested.

"I can't do that. Nobody even knows about half of what is going on," Cait said.

"Oh really? Well, you forget the small town we live in. Half of Grace's Cove is convinced that Shane kicked you out of the building. The other half is convinced that you have no money. Then there are the whispers that Shane cheated on you with Ellen and your heart is broken."

"What!" Cait pounded her hand on the table.

"Well, he has been seen kissing you around town, Cait. The assumption is that you had a huge lover's spat and now you're nursing a wounded heart," Fiona said.

"Well, that is the most ridiculous thing. Like I'd sit here and cry over a man!" Cait fumed.

Fiona raised an eyebrow at her.

"Okay, well, maybe partially over a man. This…" Cait swept her hand across Flynn's estate, "had just as much to do with baring my soul and dealing with insecurities as it did with Shane," Cait said.

"And are you done soul-searching?"

"Aye, I think I might be at that," Cait said.

CHAPTER 26

SHANE PULLED TO a stop in front of Gallagher's Pub. Cait could run but she couldn't hide, he thought. Getting out of the car, he tilted his head as he looked at the colorful building. The windows were closed up and the door, typically half open, was closed.

Shane walked to the door and saw that a small sign had been tacked to it.

"Closed until further notice," Shane read and felt his world drop out from under him. Cait was running.

"Hi, Shane," a voice said from across the street. Shane whirled around to see Patrick standing on the sidewalk, his arms crossed and his face grim.

"Patrick, what's going on here?" Shane asked as he crossed the street to meet him.

"You tell me. Did you shut the pub down?" Patrick demanded.

"No...no, I would never do that," Shane said indignantly.

"Well, it sure was weird that after she fights with your

employee in the street, she calls me to close the pub. Seems a pretty close timeline of events there," Patrick said with disdain.

"I swear that I didn't close the pub," Shane said.

Worry crossed Patrick's face.

"Is she in trouble then? Money?"

"Not that I'm aware of. Her bills are always paid on time, if not in advance," Shane said.

Patrick ran his eyes over Shane's face.

"So it must be you she's running from then. Did you hurt her?" Patrick said, raising a fist.

"Whoa, hey, no I didn't." Shane raised his hands in front of him peacefully.

"You sure about that?" Patrick asked, menace lacing his voice.

Shane thought about it for a moment.

"No, I'm not, actually," Shane said quietly. He jumped as Patrick slammed him into the wall of the market building. Offering no resistance, he allowed the young man to pin him.

"What did you do to her?" Patrick shouted.

"I didn't accept her for who she was," Shane said quietly. He watched Patrick's eyes carefully and saw the young man think about it. Stepping back, he brushed Shane's shoulders.

"That's right stupid of you," Patrick said.

"I know," Shane said quietly.

"Do you know where she is?" Patrick asked.

Shane sighed. "I was going to ask the same of you."

"She wouldn't tell me and she's not answering her phone," Patrick said.

Shane turned to look at Gallagher's Pub. It looked forlorn and just...wrong, he thought. It should be open and filled with patrons as it was every day of the week. Gallagher's was a staple in this village and very much a part of their community.

"I'll make this right," Shane promised.

"I'm holding you to that," Patrick said.

CHAPTER 27

$\mathcal{C}$ AIT SAT ON the deck for an hour after Fiona left. She watched the rhythm of the water, admiring the flow of the waves and the way the light danced across the surface. Fiona had dropped an emotional bomb on her…yet in a good way. It was just the type of kick in the ass that she needed, Cait thought, and reached for her phone.

"Cait, where are you?" Aislinn demanded.

"Shhh…is there anyone in your shop?"

"No, I'm here alone. Where are you? I can't believe that you left town and didn't tell me. I'm right mad at you, Cait," Aislinn scolded.

Cait smiled out at the water, her heart warming at her cousin's words.

"I know. I'm sorry, it was wrong of me. Forgive me?"

"Only if you tell me where you are and if you're okay," Aislinn said.

Cait took a deep breath and thought about it.

"I'm okay. Actually, I think that I'm better than okay," Cait said.

"What happened with you and Shane?"

"He couldn't accept me for who I am," Cait said quietly. This time, the words didn't hurt as much. Instead, anger began to fill the void that hurt had left.

"Well, he's an idiot then," Aislinn said automatically.

Cait laughed into the phone.

"I'm beginning to understand that. Listen, I need your help," Cait said.

"Anything."

"I want to throw a party. This Friday. A really big one. We'll open up the courtyard behind for free food and have bands all night. Can you get those bands you know from Dublin to come down? I know it's last minute."

"They'll do it," Aislinn said, determination ringing through her voice.

"Good."

"What's the occasion?"

"I suppose we could consider it a stepping-into-my-own celebration," Cait said.

"Even better. About time you shed that crap from the past," Aislinn said.

Startled, Cait held the phone away from her face and looked at it for a moment.

"You feel the same way too, huh?"

"Yup. You're the best ever and it's about damn time you realize it," Aislinn said forcefully.

"Well, this party is a start. Pull out all the stops. I'm calling Patrick next for food. Oh, and spread the word will you? I want everyone there."

Cait smiled as she hung up the phone. Forget Shane. He wasn't willing to stick around and figure things out with her...well...she'd just consider this a coming out *and* a moving on party.

CHAPTER 28

FRIDAY ARRIVED QUICKLY. Cait had spent the rest of the week at Flynn's house, planning the party from her cell phone. She trusted her friends and employees to make the right decisions. She knew the town was buzzing with the news of the party and the promise of big-name bands from Dublin. Cait didn't know how Aislinn had pulled it off and didn't bother to ask. Aislinn could be right convincing when she needed to be, Cait thought.

On direct orders from Aislinn, Cait steered her car towards Aislinn's shop and tried not to let the nerves that twisted in her stomach convince her to turn the car around. She wondered if Shane would show up tonight or if he hated her. Though he had called her several times this week, Cait had chickened out and not answered. She wasn't sure if her heart could handle him yelling at her again.

Cait pulled her car around the back of Aislinn's shop

and out of sight of the road. Getting out, she slipped through the gate into Aislinn's colorful courtyard.

With a deep breath, Cait entered the back of the shop and called for Aislinn.

"I'm here. The front door's locked, come on in," Aislinn called.

Cait walked through the back workshop and into Aislinn's store. She sighed as she saw Aislinn's latest work. Her cousin never ceased to amaze her with her myriad of talents. This week Aislinn had hung several beautifully depicted watercolors of the flowers that ranged the hills that surrounded Grace's Cove. They were heart-wrenchingly beautiful and Cait suspected they would sell quickly.

"Ais…these are amazing," Cait said as she fingered a painting of Shane's office building.

"Thanks, I was in a mood this week," Aislinn said. Cait shot her head up at her tone.

"What's wrong?"

"Aye, nothing really. Just a mood." Aislinn dismissed Cait but Cait reached out to put her hand on her arm.

"Is it Baird?"

Aislinn shrugged her shoulders and turned to stack her paint boxes. "Maybe. I don't know."

"What happened the other night? When he chased you out?"

"Saw that, did you?"

"I've an eagle eye for things that happen at the pub as you well know," Cait said.

"He kissed me. Maybe, um, more than that," Aislinn said bitterly.

Cait's mouth dropped open. The mild-mannered

psychiatrist had not struck her as the type to go after a woman that way.

"Hmm, goes after what he wants. His appeal grows. Did anything else happen?" Cait asked.

"No, nope, no-how, not going to talk about it," Aislinn muttered. Cait examined her friend's face and was surprised to find a blush covering Aislinn's cheeks. It was rare for her to be disconcerted. She wondered just how far things had gone between the two. Deciding not to press for more information, Cait ran her hand down her friend's arm.

"You like him," Cait said.

Aislinn shrugged again. "Maybe. But he's all wrong for me. I'm a dreamer and he's all but a scientist. It would never work."

"You don't know that unless you try," Cait said.

Aislinn turned cool eyes on Cait.

"You're one to talk."

"Hey," Cait said, stung.

"Well? You ran from Shane."

"Wait just a moment, he walked away from me. He called me a liar! What was I supposed to do? Stick around and grovel?" Cait demanded.

"I don't know. Maybe you should have. True love doesn't have much room for pride," Aislinn said.

Cait gaped at her.

"Love wasn't mentioned, if I must remind you," Cait said stiffly.

"Well, then, best to move on," Aislinn said quickly. Almost too quickly. Surprised, but grateful for the change in conversation, Cait nodded.

"Now, let's see this dress."

Aislinn had called to tell Cait that she had found the perfect dress for her party and Cait had readily agreed to Aislinn buying it. Aislinn had a wonderful eye for color and fashion and Cait was convinced that she wouldn't steer her wrong.

Aislinn grabbed Cait's arm and drew her over to where she had a garment bag hanging in front of a mirror. Unzipping the bag, she pulled the fabric away from the dress and Cait gasped.

"Wow, that color is stunning," Cait breathed.

"I know. It's perfect for you," Aislinn said, pride evident in her voice.

The dress was a deep emerald green, with just a hint of turquoise underneath it. It was short, tight, and with a sweetheart neckline. Never in a million years would Cait have picked it out.

"Just trust me," Aislinn said.

Cait grimaced, but agreed. She grabbed the hanger and stepped into Aislinn's bathroom. Unzipping the back of the dress, she quickly shed her clothes and stepped into the dress. Taking a deep breath, she slid the zipper up as far as she could without help.

"Need help?"

"Yes, please," Cait said and Aislinn stepped in to close the zipper.

"Turn," Aislinn demanded.

Cait turned and watched Aislinn's face light up. She gave one long, low whistle.

"Cait, you're a knockout," Aislinn said.

"Let me see," Cait demanded and moved Aislinn aside

so she could look in the full-length mirror on the back of the bathroom door.

A stranger peered back at her. The deep green of the dress was a perfect complement to her skin and her eyes popped, looking huge in her face. The sweetheart neckline made the most of her small breasts, and the nipped waist and tight skirt showed every curve of her fit body. Cait turned and peered at her generous bottom in the mirror. This dress did nothing but good things for her butt and she laughed at herself.

"I'm a knockout!"

"Wait until we get your makeup and hair done," Aislinn agreed.

Aislinn and Cait spent the next half hour going through the beauty rituals of hair and makeup. Finishing up, Aislinn stepped back and eyed Cait.

Raising a finger, she said, "Hold on." Aislinn went to a glass display case across the room and unlocked the back door. Sliding it open, she pulled out a pair of long silver earrings.

"Here. These are perfect. They're all the jewelry you need," Aislinn insisted and handed them to Cait.

"Oh, these are lovely," Cait breathed. Long silver strands twisted together to create an intricate knot. Fluid, yet interesting, they came below Cait's hair and added just the right touch to her outfit.

"Keep them," Aislinn insisted.

"I can't, they're too precious," Cait protested.

"Consider it a stepping-into-your-own gift." Aislinn smiled warmly at her.

"You can see it, can't you?" Cait said, referencing her emotions.

"Yes, I can see it all. The excitement, the anger, and the insecurity…it's all in there. But, finally, I'm starting to see your pride shine through. That's what I've always hoped for you," Aislinn said quietly.

"It's taken me a while. I'm not all the way there yet, but I'm close," Cait whispered.

"Well, tonight's as good as any to kick off the chains of the past."

Nodding, Cait scooped her arm through Aislinn's and laughed up at her.

"Invite any cute guys from Dublin?"

"Oh, yes, indeed. There's a cute guy in the first band you'll like," Aislinn said. Laughing, they left for the party.

CHAPTER 29

*C*AIT GASPED AS they got to the front door of the pub. A line fifty deep stood outside. A chorus of shouts rang out as the girls walked up the hill. Cait laughed and waved at everyone.

"If you'll just give me a minute to check on everything, we'll get started soon," Cait called.

"Damn, Cait. You clean up well," a man shouted from the crowd and Cait laughed and did a little spin.

"Don't I just?"

Cait pushed the heavy wooden door open and Aislinn followed her in. The pub gleamed from what looked like a fresh cleaning and Cait silently thanked Patrick in her head. Fairy lights were strung in criss-cross patterns across the room and every table held tea lights in lovely votives. Baskets of snacks were placed at each table and lined the bar. Aislinn moved across the room to greet the band that was setting up in the far corner. Cait waved to them, noting the banjo player that Aislinn nodded her head at. She'd be sure to introduce herself later.

Sticking her head in the kitchen, she found Patrick and her chef busy at work.

"Cait!" Patrick said and then stopped. Frank male appreciation filled his eyes as he looked her up and down. "Those no-fraternizing-with-the-boss rules still in place?"

Cait laughed and leaned up to peck his cheek.

"Yes, but thank you for the compliment. I needed that."

"You look amazing. Shane's going to grovel," Patrick said.

Cait stopped in her tracks and turned back to Patrick.

"What do you mean by that?"

"He told me that he hurt you. I made him promise to make it right. But, don't make it too easy for him," Patrick said with a grin and whisked a tray of food out into the courtyard.

"But..." Cait said after him. What did that mean? Shane knew that he had hurt her? Then why hadn't he tried to find her? Tried to work it out? Her thoughts a whirl-wind, Cait followed Patrick's path to the courtyard and let out a little crow of pleasure.

Fairy lights were strung along the fence posts here, and candles clustered the long picnic benches that had been set up. Wildflower bouquets were peppered throughout the tables. The effect was ethereal and lovely, perfect for a summer evening party.

"This is perfect, Patrick. Thank you," Cait breathed.

"Anything to save this place. We need you here," Patrick said.

Cait nodded, a lump in her throat. "I know. I'm real-izing that. Sorry that I left you guys."

"It's okay. Just don't do it again," Patrick admonished.

Looking at his watch he nodded to the front door. "Ready to party?"

"Oh yeah," Cait said and went to let everyone in.

HOURS LATER, Cait couldn't keep the smile from her face. Though she knew that the majority of opinion was that Shane was the one who had closed the place, Cait found that she didn't care that much. She never denied nor confirmed any of the allegations. Instead, she simply smiled and offered the questioning patron another drink.

Cait eyed the tables of food. Even with almost the whole village there they would have leftovers. Corned beef, ham, mashed potatoes, Irish stew, mussels in a cilantro cream sauce, and baskets of brown bread dominated the table. Bread pudding and ice cream held court on another table. Cait smiled as she saw that Fiona's famous carrot cake had long ago been devoured.

Cait turned as her name was called and her face lit up.

"Mr. Donovan!" She hurried through the crowd to where Mr. Donovan stood by his wife in a wheelchair. Cait hugged him briefly before bending down to kiss Mrs. Donovan's cheek. Cait dropped her shields so she could read Mrs. Donovan's thoughts.

"This is just lovely, Cait. Good for you," Mrs. Donovan said.

"Thank you. Um, I'm sorry about not coming on Monday," Cait said.

"That's alright. Sounds like you needed some time," Mr. Donovan said, his cheeks rosy in the heat of the pub.

"I did. But, I'm okay now. Not sure why I wallowed for so long," Cait said sheepishly.

"Affairs of the heart will do that," Mr. Donovan said with a wink.

"I told him. He turned his back on me," Cait rushed out and saw the smiles fall from their faces.

"Let him try and show his face here then," Mr. Donovan said and brandished his fist. Cait huffed out a laugh and threw her arm around his shoulder.

"No need for that. I'm going to be just fine. Better than fine, really," Cait said.

"Don't be surprised if he comes around, Cait," Mrs. Donovan communicated urgently to Cait.

"Well, then, I'll have to see if I'm willing to let him in again, won't I?" Cait said and straightened her shoulders. Looking around the pub, she allowed pride to sweep through her for what she had created here. It wasn't just another pub. This was a second home for many. Children laughed with their parents while old men told tall tales in the corner. Band number two of the night was getting ready to start and more than one person had worked up a sweat dancing already this evening. She'd done this. All by herself. She didn't need any further validation than that, Cait thought.

"You're about to find out," Mr. Donovan said and gestured to the door. Cait felt a chill ripple through her and noticed that the crowd had gone quiet. Shane stood in the door, his eyes scanning the room until he locked on hers. Without hesitation, he walked across the room.

Cait felt her pulse pick up and she took a small breath. Just being in the same room with him made her skin tingle.

Shane stopped before her. He'd dressed in a casual white button-down and jeans this evening and Cait wanted to lick the little patch of skin that showed where his shirt was open a few buttons. Pulling her mind out of the gutter, she gave him a polite smile.

"Hello, Shane. Glad you could make it."

"Cait, I've been looking for you all week. I'd like to speak with you," Shane said and swept his gaze over the avidly eavesdropping crowd.

"Now really isn't a great time," Cait said quietly.

"I can wait," Shane said stiffly.

"Then you'll be a waiting a while," Cait said. "Now, you're certainly welcome to be here but I'll have to ask that you stay out of my way."

With that, Cait patted Mrs. Donovan's shoulder and turned to go speak with the band. In moments, a jaunty tune filled the pub that had people's hands clapping and feet stomping. Cait didn't dare turn back to see how Shane had taken her statement. Instead, she smiled at the cute banjo player from the first band and slipped into the kitchen to check the food prep. There she found Patrick.

"I'll kick him out. Let me have a go at him," Patrick said.

"What! No, Patrick, stop." Cait laughed up at him and patted his cheek. "You can't kick him out as he owns the building, remember?"

"Oh, aye, that he does." Patrick shrugged sheepishly and smiled.

"Did you see that girl from Keelin's wedding is here? The one you danced with?" Cait asked, smoothly changing the subject.

Patrick craned his head to glimpse out the door.

"Is she? Isn't that interesting? She disappeared fairly quickly after the wedding, you know. I never got a chance to get to know her better," Patrick said.

"Really? I could have sworn that she liked you," Cait said in confusion.

"Aye, as did I," Patrick said.

Cait made a mental note to pick at the girl's brain. Maybe Cait could help give her a nudge towards Patrick, who had turned out to be one of her finest employees. Patrick nudged her shoulder.

"You can't hide in here all night, Cait."

Cait narrowed her eyes at Patrick and raised her chin.

"I certainly am not. Was just checking on the food is all," Cait said and swept out of the kitchen.

The crowd immediately embraced her and she shouted her hellos as she swept through everyone to get to the bar. She was about to duck under the pass-through to help with drinks when her arm was grabbed.

"I don't think so, Cait," Aislinn said. She had two glasses of whiskey in her hand. "Celebrate!"

Cait smiled and took the glass from Aislinn, allowing the heat of the whiskey to trail to her stomach. She scanned the crowd and saw the girl that Patrick liked. Leaning closer to Aislinn she nodded her head towards the girl.

"Who is that?"

"She's new to town. Working on one of Flynn's boats, actually. Morgan is her name," Aislinn said and studied her. Cait felt her stiffen.

"What?"

"Read her," Aislinn demanded.

Cait glanced at Aislinn to see confusion in her eyes. Knowing it wasn't often that Aislinn was shaken, Cait reached out and scanned Morgan's mind.

Morgan whipped her head around and glared at Cait. Cait jumped and was surprised when she felt a mental shove back. Morgan slammed her glass down and pushed through the crowd to the front door.

Cait gaped after her.

"What just happened?" Aislinn demanded.

"I…I don't know. She's one of us, no doubt about that. I started to scan her thoughts and it was like a steel door came down. She pushed me out," Cait marveled.

"Not only that, but she knew it was you who was reading her," Aislinn pointed out.

"You're right. How would she know that?" Cait wondered. She wondered if she would need to warn Patrick away from her. The girl seemed hostile.

"I had trouble reading her. Which is rare for me," Aislinn admitted. Cait huffed out a laugh at the both of them.

"Two days ago I'm embarrassed by my power and today I'm mad when I can't use it." Cait chuckled at herself and finished her whiskey.

"Here comes trouble," Aislinn muttered as the cute banjo player stepped up to them.

Cait allowed herself to smile into his handsome face and wished that he sent the same amount of heat through her as Shane did. She supposed that it would take a while to get over Shane.

"Cait, this is Declan," Aislinn introduced them. Declan smiled at Cait and held her hand a moment too long.

"Nice to meet you, Cait. Smashing dress," Declan said and allowed his eyes to trail over her body. Cait felt her cheeks flush. So maybe she wasn't totally unaffected, she thought, and gave Declan a wide smile. Declan was Shane's opposite in every way. Tattoos snaked up both of his arms, his dark hair was months past due for a haircut and his bright eyes held a wicked promise. Cait felt a low hum in her stomach.

"Thanks," Cait said.

"Care to dance?" Declan asked and gestured towards the dance floor.

Whether it was whiskey or a sincere attraction for Declan, Cait found herself nodding. She heard Aislinn's chuckle behind her and didn't have to read her mind to know what she was thinking. Girl, you're stirring up trouble.

Cait looped her arm through Declan's and allowed him to propel her through the crowd to the packed dance floor. It took every ounce of willpower she had not to look for Shane. Cait laughed as the band switched to a traditional Irish step dance. She'd grown up dancing and didn't miss a beat as she bounced up on her toes and faced Declan.

Declan smiled a challenge at her and Cait lifted her chin at him. Hands at her hips, she increased the pace. Soon, they were matching each other step for step. Cait tossed her hair and laughed up at him, enjoying the challenge. The band ended the song on a flourish and Declan and Cait stopped on the beat, chests heaving, as they smiled at each other. Gauging the crowd, the band launched into a slower song and Declan immediately pulled Cait into his arms.

Cait stiffened for a second as he held her against his chest. Deciding to live a little, she let herself relax a bit and sway to the music. A piping song of lost love swirled around them and Cait swayed, wishing that she was in Shane's arms.

A tap on her arm startled Cait and she whirled around to see Shane standing there. His eyes were dangerous as he looked past her to Declan.

"I'll have to ask you to keep your hands off my woman," Shane said.

Declan dropped his hands from around Cait and pushed her gently to the side as he moved closer to meet Shane toe-to-toe.

"Your woman doesn't seem to want your hands on her," Declan said.

"Knock it off," Cait hissed. The band had gone silent, as had the pub. Cait knew that her cheeks had to be several shades of red.

"My woman is momentarily confused. I'll have to ask you one more time to keep your distance," Shane said politely.

"Piss off," Declan said derisively and turned back to Cait.

A whoosh of air startled Cait and she shrieked as Declan hit the floor. Shane shook his fist lightly and turned to Cait, his eyes just as dangerous. Without a word, he bent and scooped her over his shoulder.

Cait felt her heart spin as her world was upended. She gasped and struggled against Shane's arms as she saw the floor pass below her. She slammed her fists against Shane's hard butt.

"Stop this immediately," Cait yelled. Embarrassment burned through her as she imagined the picture that she made, her short skirt hiked up over Shane's shoulder.

Cait gasped as applause broke through the crowd at the pub. She craned her neck to see every face smiling at her.

"Traitors!" Cait yelled.

"Give him hell, Cait," Mr. Donovan yelled.

Cait slumped down, knowing it was useless to fight. Shane carried her through the door and towards her future.

CHAPTER 30

*T*HE COOL NIGHT air touched the back of her legs
and Cait could only imagine the type of show
that she had given the pub. Hopefully, Shane's arm had
covered where her skirt had pulled up. Shane said nothing
as he carried her up the hill until he stopped walking. Cait
heard the beep of a car unlocking and a door opening.

The streetlights whirled past her head as Shane slipped
her over his shoulder until she was standing to face him.
Anticipating her resistance, he grabbed both of her arms in
one hand as he lifted her into the front seat of his car.
Reaching out, he clicked her seatbelt in.

Shane met her eyes.

"Move and I swear on everything I own that I will burn
Gallagher's Pub to the ground," Shane said dangerously.
Cait's mouth fell open and her heart pounded in her chest.
She stayed still as he rounded the car and got behind the
wheel.

This stranger, Cait thought as she slid her eyes towards
Shane's face, had replaced cool, calm Shane. His face was

tense as he pulled the car onto the street and floored it down the road, ignoring the speed-limit signs. Cait gulped as her mouth went dry.

"You had to dance with him," Shane spit out.

"Oh please, how many dates did you go on with Ellen?" Cait rolled her eyes derisively at Shane. The lights of the village sliced past their windows as Shane picked up speed and headed into the hills.

"She was my employee," Shane said evenly.

"Yeah, well you didn't mind that I thought she was something more!" Cait said.

"Forget Ellen. Where were you? How could you leave me?" Shane demanded.

Cait swore that her heart skipped a beat as a dull rage simmered low in her belly.

"Me? Leave *you*?" Cait said softly, ice hanging onto every word.

"You were just gone. All week! The pub closed. Not answering your phone. The entire town thought that I had kicked you out!" Shane shouted and slammed his fist onto the steering wheel. Cait turned and gaped at him.

"Oh, so it's the town you're worried about is it? Who gives a feck what they think?" Cait shouted.

"I do. I care." Shane admitted quietly, "My reputation as a business owner is important to me, Cait."

"Well, don't act like I purposely did this to you. You walked away from me," Cait said.

"Oh, I don't know…maybe because you dropped a bomb on me that you can read minds in the middle of my business falling apart around me?" Shane shouted.

"I didn't drop anything on you! You asked," Cait said stubbornly.

"This is ridiculous. This entire conversation shouldn't be happening," Shane said stonily as he drove into the night.

"Then why am I even here?" Cait whispered.

"Because I can't live my life without you," Shane muttered, almost more to himself than her. Cait felt a sliver of hope slip through her.

"Where are you taking me?"

"To my house. Away from prying eyes so we can hash this out once and for all," Shane said, grim determination lacing his words.

Cait turned to look at him, his face tense in the glow from the dashboard light. She couldn't go to his house. If they were going to settle this once and for all, he needed to see it all.

"No."

"No, what? I'm the driver," Shane said.

"I said no. Take me to the cove," Cait demanded.

Shane took his eyes off the road for a moment to assess Cait's face.

With a soft curse, he turned the car in the direction of the cove. Nerves twisted through Cait's stomach and she swallowed against the bile that rose in her throat. It was now or never.

CHAPTER 31

SHANE PARKED HIS car halfway down the lane from Fiona's cottage. The night enveloped them as Cait got out of the car and Shane shut his lights off. She held on to the side of the car for a moment and allowed her eyes to adjust to the soft light of the moon. The sound of waves crashing reached her and Cait drew in a shaky breath of the sea air. Soon she could make out where the hills sloped to the edge of the cliffs and the softly lit ocean that lay beyond. The moon's path trailed up the water until it hit the cove, yet the cove remained dark.

Cait tilted her head at the sight. It was the same thing she had witnessed at Keelin's wedding yet now she suspected it wasn't just a play of light. Cait jumped as she heard a bark and reached out to scan Ronan's mind.

"Hi, Hi, Hi!" Ronan panted as he raced across the field to them in the dark.

Cait bent to wrap her arms around Ronan when he pressed his cold nose to her leg.

"Hey, buddy. We are going to the cove, okay?"

"Okay. I'll come." Ronan wagged his tail at her and Cait smiled down.

"He's a good dog," Shane observed.

"Yeah, he is," Cait said quietly.

"Why the cove, Cait? Don't you think it's a little dangerous?" Shane asked. He came to lean against the car next to her.

"If you want to know me...all of me...you'll go down there with me," Cait said.

Shane eyed her for a moment. With a nod, he straightened and moved to his trunk.

"You're lucky I'm a farm boy," Shane said and popped the trunk. Cait moved around to take a peek. Inside were several pairs of Wellingtons. Shane grabbed two pairs and a wool blanket.

"These boots are a little big for you but probably better than those heels you have on." Shane gestured towards her feet.

Cait sighed at his thoughtfulness. She wondered whether, if they ended up together, his steadfastness would always complement her impulsive nature.

She slipped off her shoes and tucked her feet into the rubber boots. Though they were a bit large, she found that she could move easily in them.

"How come you have women's boots in your trunk?" Cait said, her eyebrow raised.

"My niece's." Shane smiled at her and tapped her on the nose. Cait stuck her tongue out at him and he laughed. Cait's heart clenched a bit. Maybe they could get through this, after all.

"Come on, Ronan," Cait said and together, they started

across the moonlit field. They said little as they trudged through the tall grasses and Cait's trepidation grew. She knew that she would have to perform Fiona's ritual at the bottom of the path. She squinted into the night, trying to find something to give as a gift. She could barely make out grass from a flower and she certainly wasn't going to dig up any rocks. With a sigh, she fingered Aislinn's earrings. There was really no choice but she suspected that Aislinn would understand.

They reached the edge of the cliff and both stood there silently.

"It's odd, isn't it? How dark it seems?" Shane said.

"Yes," Cait said.

"Is that…something to do with your mind stuff?" Shane asked awkwardly.

Cait shrugged her shoulders and started down the path, staying close to the cliff wall.

"Something like that," Cait demurred.

They settled into silence as they felt their way down the path, Ronan leading them carefully as they switch-backed over the cliff wall down to the sandy beach. Reaching the bottom, Shane began to step out onto the beach. Cait slammed her arm out and caught him in the chest.

"Hey!" Shane said.

"Don't go any further. I, uh, have to do something first, for protection," Cait said. Shane stared at her for a moment.

"Okay," he said quietly.

Feeling foolish, Cait slipped her boots off. Barefoot, she stepped onto the sand and drew a circle around Shane with her toe. Her nervousness ratcheted up a notch when Shane stared at her like she was crazy.

Stepping into the circle, Cait took a deep breath before reaching up to remove her beautiful earrings. Sighing, she cupped them in her palm and looked out towards the dark water.

"We come here tonight with purity of purpose. We mean no harm to the cove or those who rest here. Please accept this token as proof of our intentions. We ask for protection," Cait said clearly, though her voice cracked as she thought about what Shane must be thinking of her. With a small sigh, she threw her earrings into the water.

"Um, can we move?" Shane whispered as he glanced around fearfully.

"Yes, we should be fine," Cait said and stepped onto the sand. Ronan raced across the beach, disappearing into the darkness. Cait reached out to track him with her mind and found that he was having fun sniffing along the edge of the water.

"Will Ronan be okay?" Shane asked, worry evident in his voice. Cait smiled at Shane, struggling not to fall even more for a man that would worry just as much for a dog's safety as his own.

"Yes, the cove responds well to animals. It's just humans that it doesn't seem to like," Cait said as she began to walk down the beach.

"Why is that?" Shane asked.

Cait glanced at him in surprise.

"Well, surely you've heard the rumors about here," Cait said.

"Of course. You can't grow up in Grace's Cove without hearing stuff," Shane said.

Interested, Cait cocked her head at him.

"So what have you heard? Or, I should say…what do you believe?"

Shane stopped and unfolded the blanket, shaking it out into a large square before laying it down on the damp sand.

"Oh, I've heard that it's cursed. That people die here. I've heard tales that the real Chalice of Ardagh lies here. I've also heard that this is Grace O'Malley's final resting place." Shane paused as he finished pulling the corner of the blanket flat. "But what do I believe? I believe that there is some sort of greater power that lies within here. Whether it is enchanted…or cursed…I can't say. But, I'm not foolish enough to ignore hundreds of years of Irish mysticism. Which is why I don't come here." Shane gestured to the blanket for Cait to sit as he plopped down.

Cait stood over him, her body trembling in the darkness. It was so different for her, here. She could all but feel the pulse of magick. It caressed her skin and made her pulse beat at a different frequency.

"Do you feel any different here?"

Shane considered the question for a moment.

"I…hmm…it is almost like the air is a little thicker? Does that make sense?"

Cait smiled down at him. So, he wasn't completely immune to the magick held here.

"Much of the rumors are true. That protection ritual that I just did? For a good reason," Cait said. Unable to sit, she paced in front of the blanket. "Grace O'Malley rests here," Cait said as she swept her hand out to the water.

"So, it's true, then?"

"Yes. The reason that people can't come here isn't because the cove is angry. There is just heavy magick that protects Grace's grave."

"And the chalice?" Shane asked.

"Fiona and I both believe that it is here. But, we feel it should stay here," Cait said.

Shane sat up straighter.

"You believe that a national treasure is hiding in these waters and that it should just stay here?" Shane said incredulously.

"Yes," Cait said simply.

"I...I don't know if I can agree with you on that," Shane said.

"You have little choice. The cove will kill you if you try to go after it," Cait said simply.

Shane's mouth worked as he opened and closed it, and opened it yet again.

"Why did you bring me here, Cait?" Shane finally said.

"I'm not quite sure," Cait said as she paced. Turning to look out at the dark water, she took a breath. "Actually, I am sure."

"Okay. So, speak," Shane said.

Cait put her hands on her hips and stared down at him. "Hey, you're the one who went all caveman on me at the pub. Don't you think you should tell me why you dragged me from there?"

Shane sighed in frustration.

"Is it always going to be like this with you? A constant battle?"

Cait lifted her chin at him.

"I don't know. Probably. Is that a problem?" Cait asked. Her stomach did a little flip at him talking about "always" with her.

"I suppose that I should expect it," Shane muttered, almost to himself. Looking up, he met her eyes.

"I'm sorry," Shane said.

Cait's breath stilled for a moment.

"For what, exactly?" Cait asked.

"I'm sorry that I walked away from you. I shouldn't have done that," Shane said.

"No, you shouldn't have," Cait agreed.

"Hey, it's not like you haven't walked away from me either! That day at my stables? You just left!" Shane shouted.

"How was I supposed to stay? You didn't know me. Don't know me," Cait said wearily.

"That's bullshit, Cait Gallagher." Shane stood on the blanket and shouted down at her. Cait winced at the fury in his voice. Vaguely, she could hear the waves pick up behind her. Ronan's soft whine came to her over the wind and in a matter of moments she felt his cold nose press to her leg. Reaching down, Cait stroked his head.

"It's okay, buddy," Cait whispered.

"Oh, please. Like I would ever hurt you or the damn dog," Shane shouted and turned to the cove, where the waves had begun slamming into the beach. "Would you knock it off? I love this damn woman and am trying to get it through her thick skull!"

Heat rushed through Cait and her world did a little spin and then seemed to right itself. The cove had gone instantly still at his words and Shane stared in awe at the water.

"You do? Mind-reading ability and all?" Cait said.

"I do," Shane said.

Tears pricked her eyes. "I'm sorry that I didn't tell you. I couldn't tell you. Who wants to live with that? Knowing your partner can read your mind at all times?"

"Read me. Right now," Shane said quietly, his eyes boring into hers.

Cait hiccupped out a small sob and reaching out, she dipped into Shane's head.

"I love you, Cait Gallagher. Seeing you…being next to you…is the best part of my day. I could no more live a day without you than I could turn from you because of this. Can't you have faith in me? In us?"

Cait blinked against the tears as she shuddered in a breath. She reached deep down, scanning for anything that would say that he was lying, that he thought she was some pauper, that she wasn't good enough. Instead, she found pure, true love. Shaken to her core, she reached up with her hands.

"I love you, too. Oh…oh, so much. I was so scared that you would never see me for who I am," Cait whispered.

Shane stepped closer to her and looked down into her face.

"I see you, Cait," Shane whispered.

A wash of blue light swooped over them and they both gasped. Shane grabbed Cait to his chest, wrapping her in his arms and turning her from the cove.

"What's happening?" Shane shouted.

"It's okay. The cove glows in the presence of love,"

Cait whispered. "It's true." Together, they turned to look at the water. A soft blue glow emanated from deep in the water, its light flickering against the canyon walls, making the cove look like a giant aquarium. Ronan raced along the water and barked happily.

Cait stepped away from Shane and gestured to the water.

"I come from this, Shane. I'm part of Grace O'Malley's bloodline. Every one of us has something special. As will any daughters that I have," Cait said, watching him carefully.

The blue light didn't diminish as Shane pulled Cait back into his arms.

"So? That will just keep things interesting."

Cait laughed and then gasped as Shane picked her up and laid her on the blanket. She shivered as he braced himself over her.

"I love you, Cait Gallagher. I've been waiting a long time for you to see that," Shane said and lowered his lips to hers. Cait gasped and arched against him as he laid a whisper of a kiss across her lips.

Easing into the kiss, Shane teased her lips with his own. With a soft moan, Cait opened her mouth and Shane slipped his tongue in to toy with her own. A shot of lust tugged low in Cait's stomach and she squirmed against Shane's body, wanting, no, *needing* contact with all of him.

She gasped against his mouth as he brought his leg up between hers and pressed himself to her most sensitive of spots. Cait opened her legs helplessly, enjoying the tingle of pleasure from the pressure of his leg. With a groan, Shane lowered his mouth to the sensitive spot in the nape of her neck. Cait shivered against his lips, against the heat that trailed through her body at his touch.

Shane propped himself on his arms.

"I need you. All of you," Shane gasped out.

Cait nodded and pushed him gently aside. Getting to her knees, she pulled her dress over her head in one fluid movement. Shane's eyes drank in the sight of her naked body and he breathed out a soft prayer of gratitude.

"You're gorgeous," Shane said.

"Really? I'm kind of straight up and down," Cait said as she ran her hands along her waist. Shane reached out and grabbed her hand, pulling it to his mouth to kiss it.

"You're perfect. Every fantasy I've ever had," Shane said against her palm before trailing a line of kisses up her arm. Shane moved to kneel in front of her, running his hand along her waist, up to her bra. Leaning over, he kissed her softly as he reached around to unclasp her bra. Cait shivered as the soft breeze hit her bare breasts. Reaching out, she unbuttoned a button on Shane's shirt. Shane stopped and raised an eyebrow at her.

"It's only fair," Cait protested and Shane laughed. Standing up, he quickly stripped and Cait felt her mouth go dry as the light emanating from the cove played across the lean muscles of his body. Shane was all sinew and strength and Cait wanted to run her hands over his body. Suddenly ravenous to touch him, she reached her arms up to him. With a gasp, she laughed as Shane picked her up and slid her body down his, her breasts tingling against the hardness of his chest. Cait squirmed against the length of him. Leaning forward, she kissed the warm skin of his chest. Shane gave a soft inhale, and Cait trailed her tongue down his chest a little, tasting him, his manliness and earthiness.

She'd never felt as alive as she did in this moment. Every sensation, every touch, seemed to be heightened a million times over. His hands burned across her skin, trailing lust in their path. Her body felt liquid and loose, ready for his love. Her mind, finally at ease, was able to drink in the love that poured from him.

Shane ran his hands down her body to find her butt. He groaned as he clasped the generous lobes and molded them in his hands. "God, I've wanted to touch your bum…oh I don't know…a thousand times," he said against her neck.

"All yours," Cait breathed against his chest. She gasped as Shane stepped back and leaned down to trail his mouth over her breasts. Arching into him, she held his shoulders as Shane tortured her with his mouth, causing waves of lust to pound through her. She wanted him, all of him.

"Shane, I want you," Cait gasped.

"Not yet," Shane murmured and kissed his way down her stomach, to the sensitive V of her legs. Cait gasped as he found her with his mouth, ready and aching for him. With a moan, she cried out as his mouth took her over the edge, his arms bracing her legs as she shuddered against him, heat filling her body. Her mind hazed over with emotion and sheer delight. With a curse, Shane drew away and swooped her into his arms, laying her back against the blanket.

Shane eased her knees apart and positioning himself above her, he took her mouth in a long kiss.

"I love you forever, Cait," Shane said against her

mouth as he thrust deeply into her. Cait gasped as he filled her and then shuddered around him.

"I love you too, Shane," Cait whispered. Together they rode the wave of lust and love into completion, gasping into each other's mouths as they shattered together, finally seeing each other's love clearly.

CHAPTER 32

*C*AIT LAY ON the blanket, Shane cocooning her, and looked up at the starry sky. Her heart felt so open, so wide, that she was worried it would break. A fissure of insecurity worked through her. As though he sensed it, Shane nuzzled into her neck and kissed her damp skin.

"You know what we need?" Shane asked.

"Food? Another round? A bed?" Cait said. Shane laughed against her neck. Standing up, he picked her up and threw her over his shoulder just like he had at the pub.

"Hey, I'm an adult. I've been walking on my own for years now," Cait griped against his back, and then squirmed as she realized where he was taking her.

"Hey!" Cait shouted right before the cool, glowing water of the cove closed over her head. The shock of the cold water had her stiffening. Breaking the surface, Cait glared at him.

"I spent a lot of time on my hair and makeup you know," Cait said, treading water.

"You look even more beautiful now. A pagan sea goddess," Shane promised and dove in next to her. Cait gasped out a laugh as he grabbed her leg and pulled her into the glowing water. Together they hung in the blue glow, Cait trying to keep her eyes closed against the sting of the salt water. Shane pulled her against him, kissing her in this suspended world of magick, their love floating around them much like the blue water. Cait sunk into his kiss before he kicked them to the surface, his arms cradling her body.

Cait wrapped her arms around Shane, allowing the warmth of his skin to heat her body. The heat of his body and the coolness of the water made her want him all over again. She was about to say as much when Shane pulled her hips down against him and entered her in one smooth motion. Cait moaned as he stroked deep inside of her, touching her very core. Her muscles clenched around the length of him and Cait held on with all her might as he thrust gently into her. This seemingly never-ending wave of lust and love washed through Cait again. She writhed against him, allowing her head to hang back in the water as Shane rode her into a mind-numbing orgasm.

Shuddering against him, Cait buried her face in his neck as Shane found his own release. The cove continued to glow happily around them and Cait wanted to stay right here, cocooned in this magickal moment, forever.

A lightness filled her and Cait broke away from Shane, laughing before she dove deep into the water. The light of the water lit her path and she swam almost to the bottom. A glimpse of gold caught her eye and Cait almost swam toward it, but stopped. Keelin had told her of the cove's tricky ways. Eyeing the gold, Cait nodded at it and turned back to Shane, breaking the surface with a laugh.

"Thank you for showing me your secrets," Cait whispered to the cove and swam towards Shane, loving the feel of the cool water against her naked skin.

"Ready to go home?" Shane asked.

"Whose home?" Cait said as she wrapped her arms around Shane.

"Mine. Yours. Wherever you want," Shane said against her mouth.

"Yours is good. Plus, I like your horses," Cait said as they walked from the water. Ronan came running over to them and barked and whipped around in circles at their feet, his joy evident. Reaching out, Cait scanned his thoughts.

"Happy. Like Shane. Happy, Happy," Ronan said.

"He likes you," Cait said.

Shane stopped in his tracks and looked at Cait.

"You can read his mind too?" Shane said in disbelief.

Cait nodded and waited for the dots to connect.

Slowly, the realization caught up with Shane.

"That day in my stables…" Shane gaped at her.

"Yes, Baron told me where he was hurt," Cait said and watched as Shane tried to register the thought. A sliver of nervousness slipped through her.

A huge smile broke out on Shane's face.

"That's awesome! I've always wanted to talk to Baron. Now you can communicate for me. Oh, this is going to be great!" Shane pumped his fist in the air and, chattering excitedly about all the animals on his farm that she could talk to, he wandered away to collect the blanket. Cait just stared after him in awe for a moment before looking down at Ronan.

"And, just like that, he accepts it," Cait said.

Ronan wagged his tail against her legs and smiled up at her, his happiness contagious. With a laugh, Cait raced after Shane and into her future.

EPILOGUE

"*D*O YOU THINK she'll be okay?" Cait whispered to Shane as they packed the rest of Sarah's things into a moving van. Sarah sat on the last chair in the apartment, a bemused expression on her face.

"She'll be fine. This is the best thing for her," Shane said.

"Mom, it's time to go," Cait finally said and walked over to crouch in front of Sarah. Recognition barely flitted through her eyes as she looked down at Cait.

"Okay, dear," Sarah said easily and got up. Cait helped her down the steps and into the front seat of the van. Cait got in the back and Shane got behind the driver's wheel.

"Where are we going?" Sarah asked brightly.

"On an adventure," Shane promised and Sarah laughed freely.

"I love adventures!"

Cait closed her eyes against the tears that found their way there. She stared out the window as Grace's Cove flashed past her.

It had been two months since that life-changing night at the cove with Shane. Little had changed in her world, yet in the same breath, everything had changed. Her days were now filled with laughter and light, the occasional argument, as was wont to happen with her and Shane, and oh so much love.

Cait peered up at her mother. Fiona had been right about Sarah. Her mental condition had deteriorated quickly. In a weird way, it had also freed her. In her dementia, Sarah and Cait's relationship had blossomed into one of love and laughter. It had taken losing her mind for Sarah to let go of her negative outlook and now she embraced life with an ease that she had never had before.

Cait gulped. It would be hard for her to put Sarah in this assisted-living facility, but she knew it was for the best. With 24-hour assistance, Sarah wouldn't be a danger to herself.

An hour later, they pulled into Sunnyslope's beautiful facilities. Shane had found the center and was generously paying for full room and board for Sarah. It still burned a bit that Shane was paying and Cait wasn't. He had called it an early wedding gift and she had laughed at him. They weren't even engaged yet. Somehow, she would figure out a way to pay him back.

Cait helped her mother from the car and together they walked into the front lobby and were directed to Sarah's new apartment. Similar in size to her last place, it held a small kitchenette, minus the stove, and a living room and bedroom. The large windows overlooked a thriving garden and the green hills beyond.

Cait smiled when Sarah gasped at the room.

"This is for you, Mom," Cait said.

"This is beautiful! Oh, my shows," Sarah said and stood awkwardly before the television. There was no chair for her to sit in. Distress crossed her face as she looked around.

"Here you are, Mrs. Gallagher," Shane said as he came through the door with Sarah's favorite armchair. Setting it down in front of the television, Shane helped Sarah to sit and turned the channel to her favorite soap. In a matter of moments, Sarah was clapping her hands and laughing at the television.

The man didn't miss a trick, Cait thought, and smiled at Shane, hopelessly in love with him. Shane smiled back at her and ran his finger down her face.

"We have a date at the pub tonight," Shane said. He had insisted that she close the pub, and as it was a Sunday night, she'd agreed.

Cait went over to her mom and crouched in front of her.

"I'll come to visit often. You'll be happy here," Cait said and hugged her, trying not to cry.

Sarah smiled and patted her on the arm.

"Shh, don't cry, it's not good for the baby," Sarah said.

Cait's heart skipped a beat and she shot a glance to the door where Shane talked to the nursing assistants. Thank God, he hadn't heard, Cait thought. She'd only just confirmed that fact for herself this morning. Sarah must have picked up on it when she touched Cait's arm.

"I won't, Mom. I'll see you soon," Cait said and went to meet Shane.

On the drive back, Cait debated telling him a million different ways but no words came out. She knew that this had happened from their impetuous night of lust at the cove. Since then, they'd been more careful with their precautions.

Shane pulled to a stop in front of the pub.

"Why are we here?"

"Come on, I have something to show you," Shane said. Getting out of the moving van, he came around the hood of the car and opened the door for Cait. Smiling, she looked up at him.

"No mind reading! Promise," Shane said sternly.

"I told you that I rarely do that," Cait complained as he took out the keys to unlock the front door of the pub, ushering her in front of him. Cait came to a halt.

One of the small tables sat in the middle of the floor, nothing around it. A small envelope lay amid a circle of small candles. Cait gaped at the pub. Candles were every-where...on every available surface.

"What is this?" Cait whispered. Her heart thudded in her chest and she felt the blood rush from her face. Shane nudged her in the back.

"Go on, open it," Shane said.

Cait crossed the room and stood before the table, looking down at the envelope. Finally, with trembling hands, she reached out and opened it, sliding a piece of paper out.

"Deed to the property at 232 Main Street," Cait read and then saw her name listed under property owner. Her heart skipped a beat and she whirled around to see Shane on his knee on the floor, a box in his hand.

"Shane! Wait, what are you doing?" Her emotions in a whirlwind, Cait trembled as Shane smiled at her.

"I love you. All of you. Your stubbornness, your grit, your light and laughter. I want it all with you, Cait Gallagher. Businesses, babies, family...will you marry me?"

Clutching the deed to Gallagher's Pub, which was now legally hers, Cait stared blindly at Shane as happiness threatened to burst her heart open. Nodding, she ran to him and wrapped her arms around his neck, catching his lips in a breathless, teary kiss.

"Yes, a million times yes," Cait said against his mouth. Shane laughed into her mouth as he swung her in a circle and walked her across the pub and into the courtyard. Cait jerked as a round of applause hit her.

"She said yes!" Shane shouted to the crowd that waited there.

Cait stood dumbstruck as she looked into the faces of all of her friends and family. The Donovans cheered in a corner, holding hands. Fiona smiled at her and wiped a tear from her eye. Fairy lights ringed the courtyard and a table laden with food ran along one line of fence. Somehow, Shane had managed to surprise her, the one who could read minds, Cait thought happily.

Deciding she needed to one-up him, Cait stood back and turned to everyone.

"Well, since we are in the nature of surprising people tonight, I suppose that I can do the same..." Cait turned to Shane. "Dad."

She laughed as Shane's mouth dropped open and his

eyes dropped to her stomach. Cheers rose as Shane dropped to his knees and kissed her stomach.

"Really?" he said, looking up at her, love ringing true in his eyes.

"Really," Cait said and bent to kiss him, all the parts of her world falling neatly into place.

"Oh, she's going to be trouble," Shane said and Cait laughed.

"Nothing we can't handle."

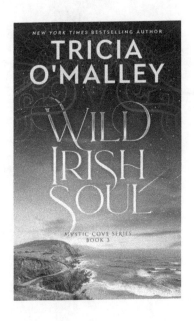

Available now as an e-book, paperback or audiobook!!!
Available from Amazon

The following is an excerpt from Wild Irish Soul

Book 3 in the Mystic Cove Series

CHAPTER 1

"AISLINN, WAIT!"

Aislinn swore under her breath as Baird yelled to her from the door of Gallagher's Pub. Pasting on a polite smile, she turned to face him.

Baird Delaney. Tall, dark and yum is how Cait had described him and Aislinn couldn't agree more. Or maybe it was the wire-framed glasses that had sunk her. Baird had come into her shop earlier this week to pick up some art for his new psychiatry office and Aislinn's world had shifted.

"Sorry, Baird, I didn't mean to duck out, but I've had a long week," Aislinn said smoothly as she clenched her fingers around her purse. All of Baird's heat and glow seemed to pulse at her and it was almost like looking into the sun. Aislinn squinted and put her mental shields up, trying to act normal.

"Ash…can I call you that?" Baird stopped and asked politely, twisting Aislinn's heart even further.

"Sure, thanks for asking," Aislinn said demurely and tried not to look directly at the smoky grey eyes fringed by the darkest lashes she'd ever seen. To keep her mind from the tight body packed into the black t-shirt he wore, Aislinn tried to place a name to the color of his eyes. Graphite? No, too dark. Slate? No, still too dark. Sleet.

"Ash? Hello?"

Startled from her thoughts, Aislinn blushed. She wanted to kick herself for blushing. She never got like this.

"Sorry, what were you saying?"

A slow smile crept across Baird's face, almost as if he knew where her train of thought had gone.

"I wanted to know where you were going. It isn't that late."

"Ah, well, you know running a business can be taxing, I had wanted to get up early to finish some projects." Aislinn said on a rush of breath.

"But the main band hasn't started yet. I was hoping you would dance with me," Baird said and stepped closer to Aislinn. The punch of him almost made her dizzy and Aislinn did her best not to step back.

"Another night," Aislinn whispered, helpless not to stare at his mouth.

"Am I reading this wrong? I was quite certain that there was an attraction here," Baird said directly and Aislinn jumped. Leave it to a psychiatrist to be open with his feelings, she thought.

"I just…I just have too…" Aislinn trailed off lamely as

she stared into his face. His very essence seemed to hypno-
tize her and helpless to stop herself, she closed the distance
between them and brushed a kiss across his lips.

A flash of heat, of rightness, seared her and Aislinn
stumbled back quickly.

"Oh no you don't," Baird said quietly and grabbed her
arms, pulling her close until her breasts brushed against his
hard chest.

Aislinn trembled against Baird as he took her lips with
his own, nibbling ever so softly. She sighed into his mouth
as he seduced her with his kiss, coaxing her to open to
him, to give just a little more. Soon, she found herself all
but wrapped around him as their kiss intensified. Aislinn
moaned into his mouth just as a wolf whistle broke their
embrace.

Unable to look at the person who whistled, Aislinn
stared at Baird's chest, happy to see that it was heaving just
as much as hers was. She couldn't bring herself to meet his
eyes. Neither said a word.

Reaching a decision, Aislinn sighed and took his hand.

"Take me home with you."

"What? No. I'd like to take you on a date is what I'd
like to do," Baird said stiffly, his honor clearly offended.
For some reason, it delighted Aislinn and she laughed up
into his handsome face.

"By the book, are you?"

"Not always, but in this instance, yes," Baird said.

"Don't you want to live a little, Doctor?" Aislinn said
and raised an eyebrow at him. She was enchanted when
she saw a blush heat his cheeks.

"It's not that I don't want to live a little, it's that I want you to take me seriously," Baird said quietly.

Continue reading Wild Irish Soul.
Available from Amazon

AFTERWORD

*I*reland holds a special place in my heart – a land of dreamers and for dreamers. There's nothing quite like cozying up next to a fire in a pub and listening to a session or having a cup of tea while the rain mists outside the window. I'll forever be enchanted by her rocky shores and I hope you enjoy this series as much as I enjoyed writing it. Thank you for taking part in my world, I hope that my stories bring you great joy.

CAIT GALLAGHER, of Gallagher's pub has lovingly put together a collection of free recipes for you. Remember to add a sprinkle of magick from Grace's Cove to make it taste just right. Join our little community by signing up for my newsletter and get your recipe book below.

Get your free recipe book here

https://offer.triciaomalley.com/shihokri9m

THE MYSTIC COVE SERIES

Wild Irish Heart

Wild Irish Eyes

Wild Irish Soul

Wild Irish Rebel

Wild Irish Roots: Margaret & Sean

Wild Irish Witch

Wild Irish Grace

Wild Irish Dreamer

Wild Irish Christmas (Novella)

Wild Irish Sage

Wild Irish Renegade

Wild Irish Moon

"I have read thousands of books and a fair percentage have been romances. Until I read Wild Irish Heart, I never had a book actually make me believe in love."- Amazon Review

Available in audio, e-book & paperback!

THE ISLE OF DESTINY SERIES

ALSO BY TRICIA O'MALLEY

Stone Song

Sword Song

Spear Song

Sphere Song

A completed series.

Available in audio, e-book & paperback!

"Love this series. I will read this multiple times. Keeps you on the edge of your seat. It has action, excitement and romance all in one series."

- Amazon Review

THE WILDSONG SERIES

ALSO BY TRICIA O'MALLEY

Song of the Fae

Melody of Flame

Chorus of Ashes

"The magic of Fae is so believable. I read these books in one sitting and can't wait for the next one. These are books you will reread many times."

- Amazon Review

Available in audio, e-book & paperback!

Available Now

THE ALTHEA ROSE SERIES

ALSO BY TRICIA O'MALLEY

One Tequila

Tequila for Two

Tequila Will Kill Ya (Novella)

Three Tequilas

Tequila Shots & Valentine Knots (Novella)

Tequila Four

A Fifth of Tequila

A Sixer of Tequila

Seven Deadly Tequilas

Eight Ways to Tequila

Tequila for Christmas (Novella)

"Not my usual genre but couldn't resist the Florida Keys setting. I was hooked from the first page. A fun read with just the right amount of crazy! Will definitely follow this series."- Amazon Review

Available in audio, e-book & paperback!

ALSO BY TRICIA O'MALLEY

STAND ALONE NOVELS

Ms. Bitch

"Ms. Bitch is sunshine in a book! An uplifting story of fighting your way through heartbreak and making your own version of happily-ever-after."

~Ann Charles, USA Today Bestselling Author

Starting Over Scottish

Grumpy. Meet Sunshine.

She's American. He's Scottish. She's looking for a fresh start. He's returning to rediscover his roots.

One Way Ticket

A funny and captivating beach read where booking a one-way ticket to paradise means starting over, letting go, and taking a chance on love…one more time

10 out of 10 - The BookLife Prize

Pencraft Book of the year 2021

AUTHOR'S NOTE

Thank you for taking a chance on my books; it means the world to me. Writing novels came by way of a tragedy that turned into something beautiful and larger than itself (see: *The Stolen Dog*). Since that time, I've changed my career, put it all on the line, and followed my heart.

Thank you for taking part in the worlds I have created; I hope you enjoy it.

I would be honored if you left a review online. It helps other readers to take a chance on my work.

As always, you can reach me at
info@triciaomalley.com
or feel free to visit my website at
www.triciaomalley.com.

Author's Acknowledgement

A very deep and heartfelt *thank you* goes to those in my life who have continued to support me on this wonderful journey of being an author. At times, this job can be very stressful, however, I'm grateful to have the sounding board of my friends who help me through the trickier moments of self-doubt. An extra-special thanks goes to The Scotsman, who is my number one supporter and always manages to make me smile.

Please know that every book I write is a part of me, and I hope you feel the love that I put into my stories. Without my readers, my work means nothing, and I am grateful that you all are willing to share your valuable time with the worlds I create. I hope each book brings a smile to your face and for just a moment it gives you a much-needed escape.

Sláinte, Tricia O'Malley

Printed in the USA
CPSIA information can be obtained
at www.ICGtesting.com
LVHW040159100524
779896LV00018B/50